High Times in the Low Parliament

ALSO BY KELLY ROBSON

Alias Space and Other Stories
Gods, Monsters, and the Lucky Peach

HIGH TIMES IN
THE LOW PARLIAMENT

KELLY ROBSON

A TOM DOHERTY ASSOCIATES BOOK

NEW YORK

HIGH TIMES IN THE LOW PARLIAMENT

Cover art and design by Kate Forrester

A Tordotcom Book
Published by Tom Doherty Associates
120 Broadway
New York, NY 10271

www.tor.com

Tor® is a registered trademark of Macmillan Publishing Group, LLC.

ISBN 978-1-250-82453-0 (ebook)
ISBN 978-1-250-82302-1 (trade paperback)

First Edition: 2022

For Margo MacDonald, with much love

1

Lana Baker was the finest scribe in Aldgate, but it won her little praise. Certainly none from her mother or sisters, who would have preferred another strong hand at the ovens. She was excused from keeping the books for their busy East London bakery, because though she could pen numbers in columns straight and square, she was a dunce at sums. Always had been. She took great care never to improve.

When forced, she wrote her mother's letters. Ran errands for her sisters in exchange for favors. Stayed out late, slept later, and thoroughly enjoyed her role as family despair.

Many, if not most afternoons, Lana could be found at the Twin Pumps, holding shop with a cup of ale at her elbow. If you wanted a pretty letter, it cost a penny a page, but for a promise, a favor, or a compliment, Lana might be persuaded to pick up her pen and write you a note. She wouldn't write curses, not for any money, but she'd put your name on a scrap for free. Always happy to show off her collection of pens and inks—especially if the girl was pretty.

The girl sitting across from her on a fine spring morning was very pretty, but she'd had some hard luck recently. A livid bruise bloomed across her jaw and nose, and her right hand was bandaged into a stump at the end of her smooth, plump arm.

"I wish I could pen the response myself," Cora said. "But I never learned ambi-hand, and if a scribe can't write her own letter, oughtn't she have someone truly skilled do it?"

Lana pretended to blush. She reached for the letter Cora had placed on the table.

"May I?" she asked.

Cora set down her cup of wine and leaned close, making the most of her big brown eyes. Did she flutter her lashes? Must be some trick of the light, for who could flirt the day after breaking a hand and bashing her face in? But then, perhaps it was a swindle, the bruise a beetroot stain. No matter. As long as Lana wasn't the mark, it was no business of hers.

"This is nice paper," Lana said, enjoying the texture of the thick, smooth sheet between her fingers.

Lana released the crisp folds and scanned the letter. A fairy summons, in an ornate uncial script inked by a skilled hand and, as with everything fairies touched, scattered with glittering scales that clung to everything. The wording was officious, with a short deadline for reply and too many official stamps to count.

Cora sighed.

"It's an honor to be summoned to Parliament. I do so wish I could go." She looked about to cry. "But it'll be months until I can hold a pen again."

Swindle or no swindle, Cora was pretty and also a fellow scribe, so to Lana that meant only one thing: the opportunity to show off. She flipped open the lid of her writing kit, selected a piece of her finest paper, and lined it with a few light passes of charcoal along her ruler. She dipped her favorite pen in a noggin of ultramarine ink.

Lana had a connoisseur's taste for admiration, but Cora laid it on a bit thick, leaning over the table and making admiring noises over every stroke of the pen. Lana could hardly fault her; she was awfully handsome, after all. But when Lana had finished the letter, stamped the corner with her mark, folded it close into a tight package, and addressed it with a flourish, that's when the price came.

"Would you run it along to Ludgate for me?" Cora laid her good hand on Lana's wrist and leaned close. "As a favor, one scribe to another?"

"Well, now," Lana said. "I might be persuaded."

"I'll make it worth your time."

Cora slid round to Lana's side and slipped her fingers featherlight up Lana's thigh. A lengthy negotiation followed, flavored with wine and cushioned with lips soft as promises. Heat rose on Lana's cheeks, neck, breast, and elsewhere. One of the reasons she didn't hold shop at the Twin Pumps more often was that the benches were too hard, but suddenly, they didn't seem hard at all. She was prepared to sit there till doomsday, if possible, kissing Cora. Then a wet rag hit her in the side of the head.

"Go outside or take her upstairs," the landlady said. "Nobody buys pies while you're turning their stomachs."

Cora pulled away. She grazed her lips across Lana's cheek and nibbled her earlobe.

"Take it to Ludgate, yes?" she whispered.

She didn't wait for an answer. When Lana opened her eyes, the hem of her short skirt was just disappearing out the door.

"Kisses will be your downfall," the landlady said.

"Never." Lana laughed. She capped her ink and squared away her kit. "Kisses are life."

"And death, too," said the landlady. "Only such as you think it's a fair way to go."

~

A stroll through East London on a warm evening. What could be better? The city burbled with activity, much of it pointed in her direction. Lana could stop at the inker's, test the newest formulas. She could nip into a penmaker's, ogle gracefully turned shanks and shiny nibs, then pop next door to the papermaker's and get treated like a hero for the price of one full sheet. The city was hers, and she was the city's. The finest scribe. Her mother's happiest and most despaired-of daughter. Benevolent and undemanding surveyor of all.

At the bakery on Wood Street, Lana bought a cream bun before turning up Ludgate. As she ascended the hill, the sun dipped to setting, throwing amber light cross the chimney stacks. Children hid from their mothers, sweethearts clutched each other in doorways, and Lana bit into her snack.

The baker was generous with her cream, far more than Lana's mother, and the bun left a dab on her nose. If only she had a friend nearby who would offer to lick it off, but no. She flicked it with her forefinger and dropped the drip on her tongue. Maybe tomorrow, Cora would offer more thanks for favors rendered. Or her childhood friend Felicia might decide to cross the street and claim some kisses. Or if the burly brewer's assistant newly hired at the Twin Pumps hadn't already found an admirer for her broad shoulders and thick wrists, Lana might console her for an evening.

Lana pondered these happy thoughts all the way to Ludgate. High atop the watchtower that bordered Newgate and New Change sat a pink fairy, small as a toddler and half as wide, if you didn't count her peony-colored butterfly wings. She had her elbows on her knees and her chin in her hands.

"Good evening, beauty," Lana caroled. She swung her fingertips to her eyebrow in a sloppy salute.

The fairy returned the gesture, not in kind, not even in spirit: two fingers shaped into horns, hooking in the rudest of gestures. It was only to be expected. Fairies were nasty. A girl could go begging for a kind word.

"And a good night to you, too, beauty," Lana sang as she passed.

On the crest of the hill, a great bloom of sunset illuminated London's fairy palace. A famous sight, commemorated in the window of every second print shop, its crystal arches and towers made only more stunning by contrast with the coalfield it sat upon. Two hundred and fifty years hadn't cleaned the evidence of conflagration from the ground below. The rest of the city might be renewed six or eight times since the great fire of 1666, charred beams and blackened foundations long cleaned away or built over, but at Ludgate, the ground hadn't changed. Neither had the fairies that came to live there. They remained as sour as ever.

Lana climbed up to the palace's rose quartz eastern door. No knocker to bang on, no porter to greet. She stood tall and lifted Cora's letter.

"I have a missive. Who will take it from me?"

A spy hole grated open. A tiny face poked through. Delicately etched features, arching brows, narrow eyes of topaz, and skin of watered silk. And teeth: sharp, bared.

"Damn you, legger," the fairy said. "Should we all come running when you call? Tell me who it's for."

"Let's see." Lana tipped the letter and read the direction. "Most Bounteous Beauty Masterwort, Director Legate of the Low Parliament Delegation from Angland." Lana shrugged. Fairies liked their titles. It was nothing to her. "Director Masterwort is resident in London, I believe. May I leave the letter with you, beauty?"

"Cool your heels, waster."

Lana flipped the tails of her coat and sat. The palace steps offered a view over the chimneys and water towers down to the river, where masts danced in a gentle tidal swell. A tidy view. Not one misrepaired or unsightly building—the fairies wouldn't stand for it. No tanneries or fishworks across the river, either, just the vast Bankside farms that grew flowers for the palace.

Lana could just make out a flower barge loaded full to tipping with tulips and making a diagonal toward Pauline Wharf. Depending on how long the fairies kept her waiting, she might see a mountain of flowers loaded onto the chain and dragged on rails into the palace's receiving gate. That would be a sight.

When the crystal door finally opened, a large apricot fairy flew out to hover at the top of the stairs, wings ablur. Her mouth was screwed up as if ready to vomit.

"I'm Masterwort. Give me the bloody damned letter," she said, her voice like crisp, rustling autumn leaves.

Lana offered the letter with a grin and a bow. It would be wrong to say she loved a challenge, for she certainly didn't, but she liked to keep genial while others brewed storm clouds. And she'd had a lot of practice.

Masterwort ripped the letter open. She sighed as she read it, then groaned and beat the heel of her fist into her forehead. Her wings shed apricot glitter. The breeze picked it up and blew it onto the coalfield, gilding the ashes.

"Damn it!" the fairy yelled. "Damn you, damn everyone!"

Lana kept a straight face as the fairy flew in circles, ripping the letter to bits. An entertaining sight, and Lana wasn't the only one enjoying it. Attracted by the fuss, the neighborhood had assembled to watch—mothers, girls, and children stood in the doorways of the printers' shops and bookstores, and hung out of the windows of their homes above. They smiled and whispered, though nobody dared laugh. A fairy tantrum might not be rare, especially for those who lived near the palace, but it was always a sight to see. Better than a street fair or a night at the theater.

When the fairy began to calm down and the entertainment was over, Lana saluted and hopped down the steps.

"Wait," the fairy said. Lana turned on her heel, smiling widely. Masterwort brandished a tattered scrap of letter. "Are you a scribe? These scribbles are your hand?"

"I'd hardly call them scribbles, but yes."

The fairy buzzed close and pointed at Lana's nose.

"And is this your face?"

"Same as my mother grew it, beauty."

"You speak Fairy well enough. Anything else?"

Lana tried to look modest.

"I learned Anglish at my mother's knee. I'm from Aldgate,

so I speak Flemish and Français. I have a bit of Gael and Cornish, and a smattering of Suomi, which I picked up from some obliging girls last—"

"Shut up."

Lana bit her lip to keep from laughing. But what the fairy said next took all humor out of the moment.

"You're going to the Low Parliament in Cora's place, legger."

"Oh no, I don't think so," Lana stammered. "My mother—"

"Lana Baker, Scribe Aldgate." The scrap of letter in the fairy's hand had Lana's stamp, iris purple on paper turned golden in the light of the setting sun. "I know your kind. Your mother'll be glad to be rid of a burden."

"I'm her favorite." A lie, and a desperate one.

"You?" Masterwort gnashed her teeth. "You're nobody's favorite anything and never will be. Pack your bags. Go to Parliament and rot."

The fairy darted into the palace, and the door slammed behind her. Lana looked around for help. The neighbors were still watching, but Lana saw no friends there. Not that they could do anything, but a little sympathy would have been nice.

"Don't try smashing your fingers to get out of it," the fairy yelled through the spy hole. "You'll go to Parliament even if I have to send your corpse."

Lana trudged beside the glassed-over drain coursing down the middle of Cheap, watching the filthy water rush to the sump at the foot of Cornhill. Now her ambitions were going the same way. What ambitions, one might ask? Well, Lana might have dug some up eventually, given soft soil and a sharp enough spade.

The landlady of the Twin Pumps had been right, after all. Kisses had doomed her. And romantic as she was, Lana couldn't pretend they'd been worth it.

2

Lana never made it home. She found a tavern on Fish Street and got sodden. Normally in such a situation, some mother would exercise her authority and send her to bed while she could still walk, but Fish Street was just uphill from the bridge, the haunt of travelers and strangers, and authority was loosely applied. Mothers didn't waste their time there, and the landlady was a happy old girl whom nobody had dared send to bed for decades.

The tavern claimed to never close. Lana proved it by drinking till dawn, and when her sister Olive found her, she was still carousing. Pens scattered. Bits of paper soaking up splashes of beer and spirit. Rude sketches flapping from the nailheads of the wall she leaned on. Lana had a pencil in her teeth and one last groat to spend.

"I'm not going nowhere," she slurred.

Olive didn't reply. She corked the inks, gathered up the bits and pieces, and tossed it all in Lana's kit. When she wound Lana's arm around her shoulders and lifted her from the bench, Lana didn't have the strength to resist.

"Will you miss me?" Lana asked, her head lolling against her sister's neck.

"Sure," Olive said. "Especially on winter nights. You're warm."

"That's all I am to you?"

Olive pursed her lips, pondering.

"You make us laugh, I'll give you that."

A syrupy giggle escaped from Lana's throat. She pulled away and tried walking on her own, then collapsed back into her sister's arms.

"Nobody's laughing right now, though," Olive said.

When they got home, everyone was busy ignoring her. Mother at the ovens, sisters kneading dough, raking coals, and sweating in the scullery.

Someone had nailed the Low Parliament summons on the pantry door next to the inventory list as if Lana were a tub of lard or jar of honey, but she made no complaint. She sat on a stool and made no fast moves until everyone's backs were turned. Then she grabbed her kit and soft-footed upstairs to her mother's room.

Quietly, quietly, she slid a leather-buckled chest from beneath her mother's bed and flipped the lid open. Inside was a wooden bowl sprouting with grains of dry yeast. Quick as she could, considering her fingers were shaking with fatigue and clumsy from drink, she screwed the decorative finials from the shafts of her pens and filled the center hollows with golden yellow grains.

This batch of yeast was the family's finest treasure, but Mother would never miss what Lana took. Yeast multiplied; that's what it was for. Lana lowered her head to the bowl and blew. One sugary breath would be enough to keep it budding until the next time her mother came to fetch a cupful.

When she was done, Lana slipped downstairs. She sat on her stool like she'd never left and announced her intent to go to Parliament with dignity.

"You'd better pack, then," her mother said, and double-fisted four loaves of bread from the oven.

What do you pack for a life of exile? Your treasures, for certain: An ancient Easter medal perhaps, the rude silver worn smooth from praying. The ribbon from your sweetheart's hair, or a silhouette of your dear old grandmam. Maybe the flower from your conception day, tossed by a fairy from high atop the local baby shrine. Your thankful mother dried it above the hearth, but now it's crumbling to dust in the bottom of a flimsy paper box.

Lana packed none of these. She gathered all the empty jugs she could find, stumbled over to the Twin Pumps, and asked the landlady to fill them up.

"For Mother," she lied. "She's making spice puddings."

"In May?" The landlady tilted her head full sideways. She was barefoot in a short shift, white legs hairy, knees knobbed.

"It's a special order," Lana said.

The landlady was no fool, but she filled the jugs anyway. Spirits only, the kind that aged in barrels for years in service of getting stronger. The kind of spirits Mother kept in a locked cupboard and drank only once a week because, as she always said, a cook might taste the sauce and still make dinner, but a drunken baker burns down the city.

And a drunken Lana? She forgets that jugs are heavy when full. Conspicuous, too.

So, on leaving the Twin Pumps, instead of turning right and heading home, she turned left. Stashed the jugs in an alley behind a bale of straw and skipped home. She stuffed all her clothes into a flour sack along with her sister Bonnie's best comb and strung it all across her chest with her scribe kit. The family followed her out onto the street. Lana tried to look noble as her sisters hung around her neck and kissed her goodbye.

"Write to us," Olive said, and tucked a short roll of coins into Lana's palm.

"I'll try."

"Try hard," Bonnie said. "It's not like writing is an effort."

"You wouldn't know." Lana stared heroically across the rooftops.

"If you don't write, we'll worry," said Angela. She was the family baby and everyone's favorite, as well as Mother's best chance at grandmotherhood.

"I'll do it to please you." Lana patted her youngest sister on her head as if she were still hip-high, gap-toothed, and not a woman grown. "If they let me, which they may not."

Mother was stern, her jaw clamped and lips screwed into a twist so severe it looked like a fairy had taken residence on her tongue. Lana kissed her flour-powdered cheek.

She forbade them to walk her farther than the corner, making up a sentimental excuse. She recovered the jugs with no risk of confiscation and staggered downhill toward the river.

Truth was, Lana felt a little less like the master of the city than she had the day before. Heavy on her feet and light in the head as if the two halves of her body were moving in different directions. Like she'd been beheaded—that was it. And what better place than on Tower Hill, where all those old girls had their heads chopped off, back in the bad old days, when the Tower still stood, its walls drenched in blood.

"Here's to you," Lana told the hill's dead. She freed a jug

from her bundle and swigged it, then trudged down to the river steps.

"I'm official," she said, flapping the summons at the waiting boats.

None of the waterwomen were impressed, but Lana didn't need them to be. She just needed to get across the river for free. After some discussion in lowered voices, the eldest helped Lana into her tippy boat.

"If you puke, do it over the side," the waterwoman said.

Lana knew Southwark. She'd caroused there in her youth, when getting away from Mother had been the priority of her life. She knew its taverns and hay ricks, its elderly inns and shops. In ancient days, they said, it had been a wallow. Life had been cheap and pleasure cheaper, and the nasty old churches raked profit from it all. That reputation, along with the distance from home and few resident fairies, made the area spicy, but Lana was long over it. City beer was tastier, and who needed a long stagger home?

Southwark being an old haunt, she knew where to get a mule cart south. She picked one with a load of straw so she could loll in comfort, hiding her liquor under the bales and lying atop her clothes to block the prickles.

Late afternoon, she woke, changed carts, and moved up front with the drover, who, by luck, had little taste for strong drink. All around was leafy and green, the road undulating like a ribbon between hedgerows.

"It's like traveling to another time," Lana said. "Angland, green and storied, where the Henrys led their armies against the fanged and horned old French."

The drover looked at her sideways.

"Who taught you history?"

"Nobody," Lana said proudly. "I learned it all myself."

On either side of the wide, crystal gravel–topped road, the land was beautiful. Rolling forests and farms punctuated by tidy villages set like jewels among tilled fields. Babies slept in rocking cradles beside their weaving mothers, brats on the roadside played kickball. Above every substantial town stood a fairy tower, humming like a beehive. When the fairies came to inspect her, Lana waved her summons. The fairies spat and buzzed off.

"You could imagine that Angland had never seen strife and never will again," Lana said.

She was fully drunk and diagonal, but in no danger of falling out because the drover had taken off her belt and strapped Lana to the seat.

"That's Parliament," Lana said. She punched the drover on the arm. "Parliament keeps it that way."

"Do you think so?" The drover kept her gaze between her mule's ears. "Seems to me we have the fairies to thank for peace and prosperity."

"That's because you're a drover. You like good weather, fast roads, and wide bridges. You don't care about anything else. Out here, life is simple. Not in the city."

"City girls seem pretty simple to me."

Lana knew she'd been insulted, but she didn't care.

"I'm going to the Low Parliament." She gazed nobly through the trees toward the flatlands, or where she imagined the flatlands to be. "That's where the real work happens." She raised her fist to give the drover another knock.

"If you hit me again, I'll drop you here. Then you can see

what kind of work wolves do."

Lana shrank back in her seat.

"You have wolves out here?"

"Bears, too. Cats as high as your hip, and boars with arm-long tusks. So if you want to talk about work, how about boar hunting? Those girls get mauled."

The road wound down into a gully, steep bank on one side, long, bushy drop on the other. At the bottom, a village out of time, houses half-timbered with roofs of shingle, all surrounded by a high stake wall. The inn was the biggest building in town, and Lana was glad to tuck herself into bed on the top floor. When the wolves started howling, she told herself it was the local girls putting on a show, but the moon through the warped windowpanes cast eerie shadows, and Lana was far from home.

She slept fitfully and woke terribly hungover. The only cure for that was more drink and a bacon breakfast. The landlady gave her more bacon and bread, and pushed her out the door into the back of a new mule cart, with a new drover, and two mules who trotted as if eager to clear the town of her.

By the time they hit the great grass sea, Lana was unable to sit up. To admire the view, she had to prop her chin on the cart's sideboards. But what view? High grass on either side of the road, growing taller in the sun. She could see enough of that lying flat. Birds everywhere, loud ones, but big animals? No.

"I thought there were supposed to be herds."

The drover didn't answer, didn't even look over her shoulder, so Lana addressed her comments to the clouds.

"Great Doggerland herds of deer and antelope, far as the

eye can see. And lions. I'd like to see a lion. A great queen with a mane and teeth like daggers."

London had lions once, back when the White Tower stood and Angland was ruled by queens. A nasty old Henry kept a menagerie at the Tower, just a hop and a skip from Aldgate, and fed her wives to the lions when tired of them. The city still had lions, plenty of them, in wood, stone, and paint. Every third tavern was the Lion and Something. Lions, lions everywhere, but none Lana could see from the back of a cart.

Just as well. They probably missed the taste of Anglish.

Early evening on the grassy sea, and it was time to sober up. She turned her back on the lowering sun and squinted, searching for her first view of Parliament's spires. Nothing, ages of nothing, just flat land, flocks of birds, and the deep crick and hum of insects.

"Look the other way, sweetie," said the drover.

"So you do talk," Lana said. "Where?"

The drover pointed to a hazy blue splotch on the horizon, shaped like a mountain, its point reaching toward the waxing moon. The mules' long heads were up, great ears pointed at the mountain, trotting faster now.

"The mules are heading to their stable and feed," Lana said. "That means you live there, too. Why didn't you say?" Lana made a fist to punch the drover on the arm, but thought better of it and patted her instead.

"I wouldn't know what to say."

"You could tell me what it's like, for a start."

"The stables are good. Our oats come all the way from Alba."

Lana stopped trying. The drover was obviously one of those girls who never committed an opinion. Careful to always be measured and responsible, never risking her chance at motherhood.

As they drew closer, the haze thinned and Parliament resolved. It was like nothing Lana had ever seen. At the bottom, it was like an old castle, a girdle of walls and parapets resting on sand. High above, at the mountain's top, the spires and towers of an abbey pierced the clouds. Between, houses large and small, snaggle-roofed and laced with windows. Picturesque, but all built from the same dull gray stone. No colorful shutters or gilded spires, not even one.

"I think I'm going to like it at Parliament," Lana said, though she meant the opposite.

"No, you won't," said the drover. "For one thing, they'll take your drink away at the gate."

The mules broke into a canter. Lana tried not to panic.

"Well, now." She raised her voice over the pounding hooves. "That's no different from my mother, and I like her well enough."

"There's the other thing, too. But you already know all about that."

"Probably," Lana agreed.

A bright flash caught her eye, just a line across the horizon behind Parliament's bulk. It flashed again and then shone a steady amber, reflecting the setting sun. The mules were galloping now, heads down, reaching for home. The cartwheels threw a rooster tail of pearly gravel behind them, and the grasslands gave way to rippled sand. Here and there were standing pools, also glowing amber.

That meant the line stretching behind Parliament was water, the whole horizon wet.

"I've never seen the ocean before," she yelled.

"You're in it right now," the drover yelled back. "When the tide comes in, this road is used by fish."

"I know tides. We have them on the Thames."

"Not ones like these. My mules can't outrun them." The drover gave her a quizzical look. "I'm surprised you're so cheery," she yelled. "I thought you were sorry to come here and that's what all the drinking was about."

"Oh no," said Lana, putting on a brave face. "This is all fine."

"Really? Because everyone else wants to leave. Once they squeeze permission out of the Maréchal Assemblay, they can't run down the road fast enough."

"Why's that?"

"The fairies won't stand for hung votes. Parliament has till the new moon to solve their differences. And if they won't or don't, that's it."

They were under the battlements of Parliament now. The mules slowed to a trot as they dragged the cart up a long, barnacle-encrusted causeway toward the gates. Lana expected the drover to keep talking, but she had clearly gotten lost in her own thoughts.

"Go on," Lana prompted.

"If Parliament doesn't get itself unhung, the fairies will call up the waves and wipe the whole place off the map, along with us and everyone else in it."

3

Parliament's main allée wound uphill in a steep curve. Throw in a few brick buildings and weatherboarded shacks, and it might have been any London street, but for the ancient abbey looming overhead. Lana's head spun. The spires, towers, and buttresses above made her woozy. Even London's greatest edifices were squat by comparison. And now it was pressing down on her, threatening to slide downhill and scrape the island bare.

A vicious hangover was setting in, but at least her load was lighter. She didn't regret the remaining liquor the guards had stripped off her the moment she'd arrived, not while suffering from too much of it. But they'd taken her coins, too, and the little penknife she used for sharpening pencils. Lovely girls, all three of them, dressed in strapped leather and armed with humorless scowls. Flirting was traditional at gatehouses— everyone knew that—but not at Parliament, apparently. Either that, or there'd been a fairy keeping watch somewhere above, and the guards had to be careful and follow the rules.

She'd have to go back again in a few days and see if she could coax a smile out of them. After a bath, perhaps.

The houses and shops along the allée all looked prosperous enough. The street was remarkably clean and free of drains. Foot traffic only, and not much of it, but when a bass bell began to toll from on high, anxious women appeared in every door and window. Lana counted ten strokes. Ten o'clock? No, it wasn't that late yet, the sky only half-dark. But the number clearly meant something important, because every woman's expression turned sour. Some even broke into tears.

"Another hung vote," said a gray-haired woman in Flemish-accented Fairy. "You've come at the wrong time, young scribe."

"So they tell me," Lana said.

"Can you swim, Anglish?" yelled a shopkeeper from the other side of the street. "I hope you sink with all your kind."

Lana looked around. Yes, it seemed the shopkeeper was yelling at her.

"Anything to give you pleasure, grand-mère." Lana touched her eyebrow with a respectful three fingers and continued to trudge up the darkening street.

The shopkeeper shook her fist. Not necessarily an unfamiliar scenario, but she'd only just arrived. Hadn't even had the chance to test the strength of her credit yet, much less get into arrears.

Straight up the allée and talk to the guards at the abbey doors, that's what she'd been told. No need to rush, though. When a gap between houses offered a view of the ocean, she put down her load and watched the tide coming in. The three-quarter waxing moon turned the water silver, and at first, Lana wasn't quite sure what she was seeing as the sea rushed over the sands.

She thought she knew tides. The Thames rose and fell.

Why would the ocean be different? Water was water, after all. But here, it flowed in rivulets that widened to streams, then spread into rivers that made islands of sand. Waves lapped at the dry margins until nothing was left, turning land into a dolphin's playground.

Waves licked gently at the walls of Parliament. As the sky turned full dark, the wind rose, the sea turned frothy, and when waves began battering on the walls, Lana turned away.

The street narrowed and began ascending in stairs as it curved sharply to the left. The cracks and crannies of each step were lined with fairy dust, turning Lana's route into a glittering web. But at the apex was no fairy palace, no verdant bower or treetop aerie, but the great, heavy doors of the abbey, lit by torches and guarded by a huge grand-tante.

She was built like a slab of granite, with age-dappled forearms big as prize trout. Silver hairs sprouted from the corners of her mouth like a cat's whiskers. By the looks of her scowl, any attempt at pleasantry would bounce right off. Still, the urge to flirt was the only thing keeping Lana on her feet.

"Hey ho, grauntie. Any advice for a poor scribe newly dropped on the rock and looking for a friendly place to rest?"

"Round to the left and up the stairs," the guard growled.

"More stairs? Have a heart. I'm about to keel."

It was no exaggeration, but the grand-tante didn't care, so Lana kept trudging. The path continued up and around the great edifice. Stained glass windows soared above, lit from inside, like multicolor blades pointing at the heavens. Lana climbed and climbed, the walls of the abbey on one side and solid rock on the other—so close she could brace herself with one hand on each. When finally she reached a tall and narrow door, Lana shoved it open with her shoulder and was dismayed to find more stairs—leading down this time, and lit by guttering candles.

Wasn't there some old tale about a rock that had to be pushed up a mountain over and over again? Clearly, this was Lana's fate now, to drag herself up and down stairs while suffering from a banging hangover. But what if she refused to cooperate? There was an idea. She'd stay up on the landing until someone came and carried her down.

"Took you long enough, legger."

A fairy voice from overhead, light and crisp as tinsel, sour as a moldy lemon. Lana waved the words away. She was done for, not one scrap left to coddle a fairy. She closed her eyes and leaned on the wall, throbbing from head to toe.

"Downstairs," the fairy yelled. "Move your clumsy feet. Don't make me come sand get you, because you won't like it."

Lana rooted herself. The fairy's threats grew louder and louder until that lovely, vicious little voice howled in her ear. Then: pain. Two jolts like hornet bites on her neck and shoulder.

"Move!" the fairy screamed.

Lana moved. Only her grip on the stairway's rope kept her from falling. The fairy rushed her along, heckling, until Lana—famous in her family for having no temper at all— was ready to spin and start swinging.

Before she was driven to that extreme, the stairs ended. The world expanded into a vaulted library lit with glassed-in candelabras. Cozy armchairs scattered among the stacks. Leather-topped desks in well-lit nooks. The scent of warm wood, ink, paper, wax, and dust. Lovely. Here, a scribe would feel her skills properly valued.

"This is fine," Lana murmured.

The fairy dropped in front of her. She was large—tall as Lana's hip, with hornetlike wings in acid yellow and pistachio green. The most remarkable feature on her round, homely face were wide-spaced eyes the color of honeycomb. Her black hair was shorn jagged, and piss-yellow whiskers sprouted from her temples, each frond battered, kinked, and split at the ends. She wore a black-laced bodice over a ragged net petticoat.

"When they said I was getting a new Anglish waster, I told them not to bother. Parliament doesn't need any more of your kind. But you're here now, worse the luck."

The fairy led her to an alcove, where a librarian with pencils in her hair made good-natured, welcoming noises. She issued Lana a crimson robe and cap, and an Anglish version of the *Guide to Parliament*. It was stained and fly-spotted, spine snapped, loose pages tattered.

The librarian apologized for the book's condition.

"The Office of Engravers and Printers has been promising a new edition for ten years," she said kindly. "I'll try to find you a better copy."

"Won't need it," said the fairy. "You're all drowning soon."

The librarian stuck her fingers in her ears.

"La la la," she sang. "I can't hear you."

The fairy harrumphed. She laid both hands on Lana's back and steered her through the room and up a spiral staircase at the back of the library. Beyond, passages led to a gallery high above the abbey's nave. In the old days, it might have been a choir loft, but now it was a scriptorium. Six crimson-robed scribes lounged in various poses of boredom. Two reclined on the back bench, sleeping together in a clinch. Another was snoring on the front bench—not loud, just a faint and rhythmic whistle against the background of casual chatter coming from the great hall below.

"Make room, Raina Estrella," the fairy said, and pushed Lana in beside the snoring girl in the front row.

Lana slipped her baggage off her shoulders and collapsed onto the hard oak seat. She couldn't help but notice that Raina Estrella was sitting on her crimson cap. Lana pulled hers from her bundle, flipped back the tails of her coat, and stuck the hat under her rump. She tightened her ponytail and ran her palms over her hair, trying to tame the mess. Not the kind of first impression she wanted to make on her new colleagues, but nothing to be done.

"So," she said, trying to regain her suavity. "Are we doomed or aren't we?"

"You mean dissolution of Parliament?" Raina Estrella asked. Oh, she was pretty. Luminous skin, very brown. Curly hair barely restrained by a buttery leather cord. A scrumptious armful. "No, it's real. Sorry to be the bearer of bad news."

A pale scribe at the far end of the bench groaned.

"Shut up. Nobody wants to hear it." She scrambled to her feet and moved to the back row.

"Syrene is more comfortable believing it won't happen," said Raina Estrella. "But the deputies do. The evidence is clear. Anyone who can leave, does. More and more go missing every day."

Raina Estrella pointed her pen at the Assembly Hall

below, where politicians in purple robes and great mushroom caps chatted and shuffled papers while red uniformed pages ran back and forth, pursuing errands. Along the green leather benches, many spaces sat empty. Horsehair stuffing puffed out of the rents in the seats like open wounds.

"How do they manage leaving?" If there was a way of getting out of Parliament, Lana needed to know about it.

"If I knew how politicians wheedled out of their responsibilities, I'd be home in my mother's kitchen right now."

The fairy dropped down from the rafters, wings buzzing.

"It's no secret, Raina Estrella. Their loving mammies write heartfelt letters to the Maréchal Assemblay." The fairy pitched her voice low in a parody of human lingo. "Commodo, commodo. If you would be so good to send my lieblingstochter chez moi. Obrigado and much obliged. Estoy muy enfermo, and I must have her nurse me. Would you deny a mother comfort in her final days?"

Raina Estrella giggled. The fairy bared her fangs.

"Laugh if you can, but your mama wouldn't pick up a pen to beg for you." The fairy jabbed her finger into Lana's sternum. "And yours don't care about you, neither."

"She cares." Lana rubbed her chest. "But not much and only on alternate Tuesdays between two and four in the afternoon."

"Prime nap time," said Raina Estrella under her breath.

The fairy snapped a finger against Lana's ear. Lana flinched, but the flick hit home.

"Let that be a lesson," the fairy said, and hopped to the back of the gallery to harass the napping scribes.

At first, Lana's ear barely stung. Then it ached. Soon, it

throbbed fever-hot.

"Horrible beast." Lana fingered her swollen ear. "Thought I was rid of her."

"Hush. You want to stay on her good side," Raina Estrella said. "Bugbite is the scribes' whip."

Lana turned her attention to the goings-on down in the Assembly Hall. The great-grandmother in the golden throne on the altar, that would be the Speaker. She slumped, elbows on the padded armrest and head in her hands. A ruby-red fairy sat casually on the throne's high back, poking at her gums with a toothpick. More fairies ranged high, playing in the cathedral arches or perching on buttresses and plinths. Two sat on the arms of the Hanging Man, an ancient gilded-wood icon that hung over the Speaker, twice the size of life and ten times as gory. At the edges of the room, lamplighters were finishing the last of the dozens of lamps and candles that dispelled shadows and gloom from the great vaulted hall.

A pair of deputies approached the Speaker. The heavy sleeves of their purple robes dragged on the black-and-white tiled floor. The three politicians conferred for a long time, frowning and shaking their heads. Finally, the Speaker groaned audibly and waved them away.

"What's happening?" Lana asked. "Shouldn't they be shouting at each other?"

"There's been lots of shouting," Raina Estrella said. "They've called a break to catch their breath and will start up again soon enough."

Lana spread her scribe's robe over her knees and rested her pounding temple against Raina Estrella's obliging shoulder. When she had a problem, a nap was never out of order.

Usually, the problem was gone by the time she woke.

Her eyes drifted shut. How could anyone be expected to stay awake here, with so many voices rising from below? It was like being a child again, warm and cozy in the family nursery, listening to the hum of conversation from the kitchen, while death-watch beetles played ticktock in the rafters above.

Then the Speaker slammed her mace on the clerk's desk, and Lana lurched to attention along with the other scribes. Pages fluttered as they opened their journals, and steel nibs began scratching over paper.

Lana craned her neck to see what Raina Estrella was writing. Bugbite landed by her shoulder, little feet in grimy pink slippers gripping the back of the bench.

"Take a book from inside the desk, and scribble everything they say down below," Bugbite shouted in Lana's ear as if she were a century old and gone hard of hearing. "Don't get into a bother if you don't understand nothing but Fairy and Anglish, or if a word's too big for you. Nobody expects much from a scribe. That's why we keep a gaggle."

Lana was offended.

"My vocabulary is top-notch, thank you very much, and I know quite a few languages."

Bugbite's expression sweetened.

"What a clever tongue you must have," the fairy said, clearly impressed. "Can I see it?"

Lana smirked and let her tongue loll seductively from between her lips. The fairy's hand flashed. Lana snapped her jaws shut—too late. Her tongue smarted as if burned.

"When you don't understand the big words, just leave a blank," Bugbite said, and buzzed away.

"I'm afraid you asked for that," said Raina Estrella.

So, Lana's first hours in Parliament proceeded with a throbbing ear and a swollen tongue. Raina Estrella had been right about the shouting—and when that shouting was in a language she didn't understand—Russky, Polski, Magyar, Elliniká—she used the time to compose a letter to her mother.

Dear Mama, she penned on a fine sheet of her own best paper. *You were quite correct as always in your infinite wisdom to send me to Parliament, where I have learned much and mended my rash and unheedful ways. A note from you to the—*

Lana tried to recall the authority Bugbite had mentioned.

—Maréchal Assemblay will bring me home because you are of course quite terribly ill and require my kind hand to nurse you. I do so vow and promise that no more will you be disquieted by the lively behavior of your most engaging and devoted daughter.

Mother was terribly hearty and never ill. She would undoubtedly catch the hint, but would she understand how essential this was? Lana added a postscript.

Perhaps you have not heard that Parliament is about to undergo the ultimate proroguing. I do not mind to die and indeed would call it an honor to meet the end you chose for me. They say drowning is a kind death.

Too much? Too little? She added another postscript.

I am not exaggerating. xoxo

4

When Parliament finally closed the day's session, well after midnight, the scribes trooped down to the library, through the stacks and up yet another staircase to their own residence hall. A midnight supper waited there, cooling on a trestle table. Lana counted seven scribes in total, including herself. Didn't seem like many, considering all the hundreds of Euro tongues.

If they had been allowed to eat in peace, Lana would have asked about that, but Bugbite was playing tyrant. She stomped to and fro across the table, threatening to upset the mugs and jugs as she ranted and scolded. Nothing to wonder at in that; fairies were always in a bad mood. Once or twice a year, you might catch one of them laughing, usually at some poor fool gone head over tails, but at all other times, they were miserable.

The food was comforting, though. Eel pie and warm pickles. But what was a pie with no ale to wash it down? Supper included two jugs of very small beer. Divided among seven scribes, there was barely enough to smack your lips with.

Still, the beer was worth protecting. No scribe left her mug unguarded, or the fairy might kick it over.

"The problem with Parliament is clear," said Bugbite. "You

humans are all dumb as rocks and twice as useless. Do you know how else you're like rocks?"

"We sink like them?" Lana ventured.

"True that. But I was thinking about how numerous you are. How many babies did the natal fairy give your mother, legger?"

"Four, gracious beauty."

"And one of those a waster like you. She'll never make you a mother."

"Good thing, too, because I'll never ask for a baby. I have other sisters who are better suited for motherhood."

Bugbite ignored Lana's comment. She'd moved on to abusing the other scribes, pointing at them with her soft little nailless finger. "You're all wasters, each one of you. No human is any use. Why do we make you? It's a mystery."

The fairy launched herself into the air and buzzed out of the room. The tableware rattled in her wake.

Lana abandoned her piecrust and followed the fairy at a trot.

Her every bone ached. All she wanted was to fall into bed, but here was an opportunity. Bugbite's size and homeliness would make her an object of ridicule among fairies, and outcasts always yearned for friends. Lana still had a chance to make an impression on the fairy, and she wasn't about to waste it.

She pursued the fairy around a corner, across a hall, and through a series of dusty rooms to a wide balcony, where the fairy crouched like a gargoyle on the balustrade.

"Heyo, beauty," Lana called.

Bugbite hooked her thumb over her shoulder.

"The roof is that way. If you jump from here, all you'll get is a broken bone."

"But if I died, they'd send you another scribe. And she's not likely to be as handsome and charming as me."

Bugbite huffed twice. Lana slid her leather pen case from the inner pocket of her tailcoat and removed her carved box-wood pen. She put her elbows on the balustrade and rolled the pen over her knuckles. *Keep quiet,* she told herself. *Make her come to you.*

"You Anglish," the fairy said finally. "It's all your fault."

"Did an Anglish girl break your heart, Beauty Bugbite?" Lana asked. "Point me at her. I'll avenge you." She swept the pen like a sword and stabbed.

The fairy laughed, a harsh bark with a hornet buzz behind it. She wiped her forearm over her forehead. It came away coated with wing scales. The fairy examined the glittering en-crustation for a moment, and then flicked it away.

"Nobody else is making jokes here. They're too busy throwing away nine generations of peace and beneficial gov-ernment. Why can't you just be normal?" She spat the word like an insect had landed on her tongue.

Lana unscrewed the pen's golden finial and poured a bit of Mother's yeast into her palm. The fairy's tortured whiskers shivered. She was clearly interested.

"Perversity is the human condition," Lana said soothingly. "We simply can't help ourselves. Tell us to do one thing, we'll do the opposite every time."

The fairy's wide, honeycomb-colored eyes grew huge. She stretched out her little hand, tentative. Lana tipped a few grains into it. They touched fingers as if toasting and then licked their palms. A euphoric sense of well-being spread through Lana's shoulders, down her back, and swirled around her knees. The fairy shifted from her gargoyle position and sat, knees apart, feet swinging. When she giggled, it sounded almost human.

Soon, Lana's and Bugbite's shoulders were tipped together like a couple of old pals. When a trio of pages raced across the courtyard below, they giggled. When a bespectacled chamberlain stomped over the paving stones, they chortled. They hooted while two maids took advantage of a dark corner for a quick kiss and a grope. They heckled a Parliamentary deputy and the Speaker herself, then ducked inside to hide.

"You are a bad girl, Lana Waster," Bugbite whispered.

"My mother taught me how to make people happy." A rare sense of accomplishment spread through Lana's core and out to her fingers and toes. All was well. She'd made a fairy laugh, not once but many times. She deserved a medal.

The two of them kept up the antics until they were both boneless and droopy from all the fun, too tired to guffaw, and too lazy to go to bed. Then one last victim edged into the courtyard.

"Hush." Bugbite clapped her small hand over Lana's mouth.

A graceful woman floated into view, dressed in a plain shift and spangled slippers, her face round and shining, her wrists and ankles slender as reeds. She lifted one arm as if picking a book off an invisible shelf and then floated across the paving stones as if the imaginary book were carrying her along in its wake. When she reached the middle of the courtyard, where concentric paving stones gathered around one smooth, blue granite slab, she fell as if the book had shaken her off, then caught herself and spun, arms reaching for the stars.

Lana knew little of dance. She and her sisters had learned jigs and reels, bops and gavottes. Those bore little resemblance to the art of dance, no more than alley graffiti looked like a master portrait. But she knew genius when she saw it and recognized skill so finely tuned it edged into magic.

Lana retained no sense of time. Who could, when such glory was before her? Finally, the dancer rested in stillness on the granite slab and lifted two fingers to her lips—a benediction, a blessing. Lana and Bugbite sighed in unison.

"Who was that?" Lana breathed as the dancer disappeared through a shadowed doorway.

"Doesn't concern you. Or me either, when it comes right down to it." Bugbite launched herself off the ledge with a grunt and hovered, fists couched solidly on each hip. "But I know an Anglish waster who needs to sleep."

Bugbite shooed Lana back to the scribes' hall and into a curtained wall nook. Tired as she was, Lana slept lightly, dreaming of nightingales plucking cherries from the lips of a snow-clad dancer.

5

Bugbite woke the scribes with kindness, bouncing between curtained nooks and tickling them all awake. From the scribes' shocked reactions, it was clearly unprecedented behavior.

The fairy left Lana to last, and when she poked Lana in the ribs, her touch only provoked a tiny spark of pain. Then she waggled her eyebrows. She pulled a mushroom from her pocket and peeled a scale from its purple cap. Lana opened her mouth. When the scale touched her tongue, the room grew bright with unearthly colors. The ceiling peeled back to reveal leafy canopies buzzing with sparkling insects.

"Good morning," Bugbite said, and winked.

Breakfast was sweet gruel and tepid tisane brought by red-cheeked kitchen maids whose tightly braided hair sprouted with glassy shelf fungus. No—bevies of rainbow-hued bushtits. No—hart horns dripping with velvet that wept milk into the serving pots.

"I'm not sure I can work under these conditions," Lana said to Margit, the freckled scribe on her right. Margit yawned and wished her good morning. Then her freckles opened their eyes and winked.

When the bells called everyone to the day's session, the

scribes shrugged their robes over their clothes, shouldered their kits, and trudged up to the gallery. Lana felt mostly normal. If the bench she sat on was made of warm ice that pillowed under her rump, Raina Estrella didn't seem to notice. Nor did she object to Lana trying out the icy bench's give, bouncing up and down a few times before sitting on her hat.

Bugbite spent the first few hours up in the rafters, chewing on her nailless thumb and giggling to herself. Then, as twilight descended and the lamplighters began their rounds, the fairy settled at Lana's shoulder.

"As far as death sentences go, Parliament isn't all that bad," Lana told her. "If the beer were just a little less small, and we could have a good strong wine in the evening, I could be happy to make a career here. Especially since the girls are so pretty and obliging."

Raina Estrella blushed and giggled, fluttering her hands as if to push the compliment away.

"They're awfully kind, too," Lana added. "They laugh at my jokes."

"Raina Estrella is a philanthropist," said Bugbite. "She'll take any small offering and quadruple the value, making the original seem far more than it's worth."

When the Speaker called a recess and the deputies below got up to stretch their legs, Lana grabbed her tattered copy of the *Guide to Parliament*. She squinted at the diagram of the abbey and environs, looking for the courtyard with the blue granite center stone. But Parliament was an anthill, and no matter which way she turned the map, she couldn't orient herself.

"Is this it?" she asked Bugbite in a whisper. "The courtyard from last night?"

The fairy took the book in both her hands. She turned it this way and that, brow furrowed, clearly confused.

"Where's the rest of it?" she said, and ran the palm of her hand over the worn and ratted paper. "This is flat. The world isn't flat."

It made sense, Lana supposed, that fairies couldn't understand maps any more than fish followed roads or birds obeyed walls. But Raina Estrella did. She took the map from the fairy's hand and gave it a hard twist. She pointed out a few key features—the Assembly Hall, the scribes' hall, the kitchens, the library.

If Lana made her guess right, the dancer had come from the kitchens. Wouldn't that be luck? A potager or poissonnier, maybe, or if her luck was high, a pâtissier. Lana could seduce her with kitchen talk, promise her mother's secret recipes. But was that likely? Would a dancer of that talent work in a kitchen? Perhaps. Dancers, like anyone, had to eat, and kitchen work took endurance and strength.

Bugbite's hand dropped on Lana's shoulder. Lana followed her gaze, and the dancer drifted across the checkered floor like a spring blossom.

She was older than Lana had imagined and at least ten times more beautiful. Darkest hair glittering with silver strands, hips broader than her nightdress had suggested. Long-necked and sweet-natured—that was obvious, written on every line of her face. Full lips, fuller than Lana's cherry-stained dreams. Smiling eyes, laugh lines, and skin that caught the light from the cathedral windows and reflected it back into the room, making everything inside brighter and more worthy.

Only one problem: the dancer was dressed in purple robes. She was a politician. She took a seat on the Assembly's lowest tier, and though she could see only the back of the dancer's head, Lana was mesmerized. When the Speaker called the session back to order, Lana missed it.

"Are you going to start working anytime soon?" Bugbite tapped Lana's desk.

Lana shook herself. She opened her journal and cleared her throat officiously as if preparing to make a speech. Raina Estrella giggled. Lana spun her pen over her knuckles. The scribe giggled again.

"Bugbite is right," Lana breathed in the scribe's ear. "You're too easy to please."

As the night wore on, in between tossing jokes at Raina Estrella and Bugbite, Lana watched the back of the dancer's head. An occasional quarter profile showed the sweep of her soft cheek, the corner of her mouth, and a dimple that appeared only once but etched itself in Lana's fancy—to the point where, deep past midnight, Lana found herself composing a song, searching for a rhyme for dimple that wasn't rude.

And what did she think of the Parliament proceedings? The arguments, the motions, the posturing, the jostling for power? It didn't seem real. Just petty squabbling, like children fighting over cake. Except here, what they squabbled over wasn't even real but nuances of governance. Not voting, or how or when to vote, but whether or not previous votes counted, and if they should be recalled and allowed to vote again.

"I'm beginning to understand what's going on here," Lana said loudly. Raina Estrella was impressed. Syrene looked dubious. Vera and Margit both smiled. Melodia and Una, cuddled on the back bench, were too engaged with each other to notice.

Lana spread her hands as if encompassing all the deputies on the floor below, the Speaker, and the pages in their gold-braided jackets.

"This is an endurance trial. Whoever is most stubborn, wins."

Syrene hissed. Vera and Margit laughed.

"No," Raina Estrella said. For the first time, Lana's joke had missed the mark with her. The scribe flipped through the pages of her journal, thick with swooping script. "That's a cynical view. This means something. It has to."

Lana patted the scribe's shoulder.

"Okay. I'm new. You tell me, then, what does all this really mean?"

Raina Estrella flipped to the first page of her book and began going over the day's proceedings. The deputy from Berkingmiddleshire had dominated the day, putting forward a baffling array of arguments about ancient trade treaties and land grabs in territories that had nothing to do with Angland at all, except for claiming legal precedence. Her argument was stupid, even Lana could see that. But the deputy was old. She'd been in Parliament since before Lana was born, and judging from her vehemence and abundance of flying oratorial spittle, she was uncompromisingly bullheaded.

Lana pretended to listen to Raina Estrella. On Lana's

other side, Bugbite slouched on the back of the bench, knees high, black-and-white-striped bloomers exposed, her elbows couched on the petticoat that flounced over her knees, chin in her palm. She looked sad. But Lana knew how to cheer her up.

She reached into her pocket, twisted open one of her pens, and passed the fairy a pair of yeast grains. It put a sparkle in Bugbite's eyes. Perked Lana up, too, and kept them both awake until everyone was dismissed for the night.

Lana was eager to visit the balcony again, but after supper, Bugbite was gone. Raina Estrella had disappeared, too. Lana found them in an adjacent room, a great slant-roofed gallery with a lime-washed floor, marked up with scratched diagrams and charcoal notes. With them was a page in her gold-braided coat, and they were all talking in low voices. The page looked huffy. Raina Estrella gestured broadly, arms flapping like wings. Bugbite hovered between them, stern.

No matter, Lana could find the balcony herself with the help of the map from the guidebook. Maybe she might have found it if she'd started from the scribes' hall. Maybe. Instead, she started where she was and got helplessly lost. She'd just decided to sleep in a dusty corner when Bugbite rescued her and dragged her to bed.

6

Mushroom scales in the morning. Yeast in the evening. Scribing in between, the boredom and cramped fingers leavened with jokes, pleasant company, and glimpses of the dancer's marvelous face.

After cross-referencing the outdated seating arrangement in the *Guide to Parliament* and checking the lists tacked up in the library, Lana was able to put a name to her: Eloquentia de la Barre, la députée de Dauphine-Provence. Eloquent definitely, but not with her voice.

Lana hadn't heard her speak yet, not once. Eloquentia sat straight, listened attentively, and took notes. Her shoulders never drooped with fatigue. She never allowed herself to groan with frustration, never pounded her desk or shook her fist like the other deputies. She remained composed, poised, gorgeous.

"If she'd just open her mouth," Lana observed to Bugbite, "none of these idiots would dare let a vote hang. They'd agree to whatever she said."

The fairy blinked vaguely, her gaze focused on a point somewhere above the ceiling. It was early in the session, and Lana's vision still sprouted with hallucinogenic filigree. They'd haunted the balcony together for hours, waiting for

Eloquentia to appear. She'd arrived late and stayed long, and each step on those cold stones had imprinted itself on Lana's heart.

"I have to meet her," she whispered to herself. A crown of golden roses buzzing with glowing honeybees settled on the dancer's dark head. When she lifted a hand to settle a lock of hair behind her ear, the bees clustered on her fingers like furry rings, bestowing honeyed kisses on each of her knuckles.

"Meet who?" Raina Estrella said.

"My beloved. She hasn't met me yet, but I . . ." Lana put a modest hand over her heart. "I am her destiny."

"She's certain to love you back." Raina Estrella tilted her head at Bugbite, who was now staring dreamily into the Assembly Hall as if admiring a vision of paradise. "Clearly, you can charm anyone."

Down on the floor below, a dapper page was glaring up at Lana. Was she the same one she'd seen arguing with Raina Estrella? In their brimmed caps and heavy broadcloth jackets covered with gold braid, the pages were indistinguishable. She'd have to try to remember this one's face. Once she made Eloquentia's acquaintance, it would be helpful to have a page in her pocket for passing notes and little nothings.

She gave the page a jaunty wave, and the face under the cap crumbled into a monstrous scowl. Raina Estrella cleared her throat loudly and shifted away from Lana, then began vigorously swiping her pen nib with a cleaning rag.

"Oh!" Lana said, realization dawning. "She's your sweetheart and jealous of you and me."

Raina Estrella coughed.

"That's spicy." Lana leaned in and put an arm around the scribe's plump shoulders. "A little frustration puts frosting on kisses, don't you think?"

"Stop it," Raina Estrella said, very serious. Lana slid away and switched her attention to Bugbite.

"Will you give me a tour of Parliament tonight, BB?" The fairy's glassy eyes slowly changed focus, but didn't quite make it to Lana. "I can't keep getting lost. Have to be able to find my way around in case some other page gets a taste for scribe."

"Huh?" The mushroom scales had clearly hit the fairy hard that morning. Lana slid closer.

"You know. Romances. Liaisons. Corner clinches. I don't want to lose any chances to indulge myself in a friendly, warm bosom just because I get lost on the way."

The fairy giggled softly. She ran her forefinger along the shell of Lana's ear, leaving a zesty trail of sparks.

"I'm going to be so sad when you drown." Her lower lip pooched out and quivered. "Why can't you humans get your shit together?"

The Speaker slammed her mace hard on the table.

"Good question," Lana murmured, and flipped open her journal.

~

The deputy from Berkingmiddleshire forced a vote. Lana didn't understand the terms. Something about recognizing the special provenance of tin and granting sole right to cross-border trade in worked tin goods to Anglish and Cornish craftworks. Which meant, she supposed, that regions without their own tin mining couldn't purchase the ore but would have to import finished Cornish and Anglish products.

A stupid vote. It should have scored an easy Nay, but it hung. Deputies yelled and smashed their fists on the tables. Fairies keened, their faces spurting with glistening tears, wings stuttering and shedding scales. Even Eloquentia left the Assembly Hall looking pensive and disturbed. Supper was subdued, even depressed. The scribes swilled their beer as if any amount of alcohol, however weak, could bring relief.

Lana took a pen from her pocket and gestured Bugbite over.

"Should I pass this around?" she whispered.

"Do you have enough for everyone?"

"For tonight, yes, but then it'd take several days to re-bud."

The fairy tapped her fingers on her lower lip, thoughtful.

"Save it for another vote, I think."

Bugbite and Lana descended to the library and stooped through a low passage into the old scriptorium tower. Tall windows slashed vertically through its barrel-shaped walls. Stairways cluttered the narrow floor. Some were substantial marble or granite affairs. Some were wooden, patched with scrap and honeycombed with woodworm.

Bugbite flew high and hovered, hands on her hips, hornet-striped wings ablur.

"And so," Lana said, "what is this place?"

The fairy buzzed close and tapped her finger on Lana's clavicle, sparking nettle-like zaps.

"Totally helpless. You have no sense of direction, Lana Baker."

Lana batted the fairy's hand away.

"And so, would it hurt to put signs over the doors? Are we supposed to guess?"

"You could try."

Lana paced the room in a circle, hemming and hawing.

"Okay, which door leads to BB's secret mushroom farm?" She ran to the top of the highest stairs and then leapt over to the next. "This one?" She made another huge leap to a rickety stair. When she hit the landing, the wood gave an ominous crack.

"It's sad humans can't fly. You try so hard to escape your nature."

"I know, we're pathetic." Lana gave her friend her most charming grin. "Fine, I give up. Which way to the courtyard?"

Bugbite's wings hiccupped. She dropped a foot before catching herself.

"You mean, where the dancer goes?"

Lana nodded vigorously. Bugbite blinked three times, then slowly lifted a hand and pointed at a doorway.

"Very good. Let's catch the show up close and personal tonight."

Lana had never seen a fairy look so guileless. Her pale eyelashes splayed wide, her kinked whiskers smoothed. She ran her hands over her ragged bodice and petticoat, flattening the frayed edges.

"B-but," Bugbite stammered, "she'd be able to see us."

"And we'll be able to see her better. Come on, then."

Remember this, Lana told herself. The stairs were gray-veined marble, the center of each step worn to a curve by generations of feet. The oak door didn't latch properly and banged against its jamb on loose hinges. Beyond was a corridor between the walls of two buildings of different ages, one of solid dressed stone, the other slapped together with mismatched hunks of rubble. Moss patched both walls, except at shoulder height, where foot traffic had scraped it away. No glitter on the walls or the ground, though. Fairies had no use for it; they took the crow's road.

"BB, why do you hide up on the balcony to watch the dancer? You could jump down and say hello anytime you want."

"Why would I?" Bugbite thrust out her jaw and balled her fists. "Humans are the worst. Bad enough I have to clean up after you scribes."

A little woodpile courtyard provided no fewer than six options. Three of them were clearly kitchens, judging from the clanging, the smoke, and the radiant heat from the ovens. The bakers were at work making tomorrow's bread. Lana picked up a stick of kindling and sniffed it. Good seasoned oak, the same as her mother used. She prodded at that idea as if using her tongue to feel a loose tooth, checking for the ache of homesickness. But London seemed close enough. She could walk home if she had to. Or could she?

"Hey, now. What happened to your other Anglish scribe, BB?" she asked.

But the fairy had retreated into a mood. She wouldn't answer, and neither would she give any more directions.

"How should I know which way to go?" she grumbled. "This is a snakepath. Good only for humans and other lower creatures."

She fled up and over the roofs, leaving Lana alone. Fine. There was more than one way to get around. Lana poked her head into one of the kitchen doors and gave a halloo.

The kitchen girls were friendly, generous, and eager for distraction. Lana would have gladly wasted more time sitting on a high stool, letting them ply her with bits of this and that—a bite of salty crackling hot off the roast, a nip of carrot wine so old it was nearly syrup. She let herself waste an hour. When she pulled herself away, a cook with blond braids followed her to the woodpile and leaned in for a confidential whisper.

"Some are saying we might have to murder the deputies. What do you scribes say?"

Lana jerked away. Her mouth worked, unable to form words to make a reply.

"Were you expecting sweet nothings?" the cook asked. Lana nodded vigorously. "Who thinks about romance when the specter of death is overhead?"

The cook glanced skyward. Lana followed her gaze, and there was Bugbite, waiting on the edge of a roof, picking idly at the holes in her net petticoat.

The scrub gripped Lana's forearm and squeezed.

"Deputies aren't the only ones that need killing. Take this."

She pulled Lana in close and showed her a kitchen knife. Then she slid it up Lana's sleeve.

"Okay, then, I have to go." Lana yanked herself out of the cook's grip and lunged for a door at random.

When Bugbite found her, she was circling a series of apartments on the ground floor of a wide tower. At one time, it had been a piggery. Now it was used for storage, with broken furniture and bits of detritus piled and stacked at random.

"I found the door in!" Lana shouted. "Why can't I find the door out?"

"The door in *is* the door out," Bugbite said.

"This place is a maze. If Parliament caught fire, we'd all burn to death."

"That won't happen. We don't let it."

"Why not? You're fine with letting us drown."

"It wasn't my idea. You humans made this bargain centuries ago."

"Well, it wasn't my idea, either." Lana put her hand on her hips, mirroring the fairy's stance. "In fact, I'll tell you right now, I disagree with drowning. Most vehemently. When we get to the last vote, I'm not going to wait around. I'm leaving, and I'll take the scribes and everyone else with me."

Bugbite looked horrified.

"You can't do that," she said.

"Why not? You going to lock us in?"

"The tidal flats are full of sinkholes, mud traps, and quicksand. If you leave without permission, the road will take you right in the middle of them. That's what happened to the scribe before you."

"You let her die out there?"

"I would have brought her back safely if I'd had the chance."

Lana hooted.

"Safely? How safe is this? Parliament is a prison, and you're the wardens. We don't deserve to die."

"Stop fighting, then!" Bugbite screamed.

She slammed her hands on the wall. Sparks flew from

under her palms. When she drew away, her handprints stood on the stones, imprinted with whorls of glitter.

Lana sat heavily. She pulled out a pen and dumped a mass of yeast on her palm. Two generous helpings—why be parsimonious when death was so close? The fairy settled by her side. They licked their palms in unison, and within a minute, the world brightened, troubles lessened. Time slowed down.

"We have until the new moon, right?" Lana asked.

"Right."

"Anything could happen between now and then."

"Anything at all," Bugbite agreed.

"You and I shouldn't fight. We should live for today." Lana nodded vigorously in agreement with herself. "I could fall down a flight of stairs tomorrow and crack my head open. You could . . . die of whatever fairies die of. And then all this—" She swept her arm to encompass the pig-boards, the farrowing stalls, the cracked chairs and warped bedsteads piled high all around. "All this means nothing."

Lana slapped her chest.

"Everything that matters is right here."

"Your tits," said Bugbite, grinning.

"My heart." Lana laughed. "Your heart, too, though you pretend not to have one. Love, that's what matters."

"Love," the fairy agreed.

Lana was happy to hear her say it. There was something in Bugbite's expression, though, that made her look conflicted. They said—whoever *they* were—that love and all the other higher values were foreign to fairies, and that's why they were so terrible. Their nature was vengeful, and once crossed, they neither forgot nor forgave.

Was Lana playing with fire, making friends with Bugbite? Sitting there in the old piggery, both of them happy as Mother's finest yeast could make them, Lana couldn't imagine a bad outcome. It was in her nature to be trusting. But the cook's knife was still up her sleeve, its cool blade lying along the soft skin of her forearm, and if the cook could see Lana now, she'd call her a fool.

7

From time to time, Lana thought she'd begun to understand some of the politics at play down in the Assembly Hall, but mostly, she was completely confused. But if she went to bed baffled, she woke refreshed and ready for enlightenment. Only the kitchen knife hidden under her mattress kept her from waking in innocent comfort.

Two deeply divided factions had formed among the hundreds of deputies. When the Speaker announced a Call for Decision, the numbers of Yea and Nay were split nearly equally, with a few abstainers.

At home, in London's Worshipful Company of Bakers, a plain majority would be enough to accept or reject a decision, but not in Parliament. Here, to pass or reject a Call for Decision required a strict majority of two-thirds. Otherwise, the vote was hung.

Lana examined the voting records posted in the library. They showed that over the past two months, every single vote had hung, but lately, something had changed. Factions were beginning to split and fray. It wasn't just two sides arguing against each other anymore, it was five. Then nine. From Lana's bird's eye view in the scribes' gallery, it seemed like every deputy was a faction in themselves, confused and divided not only from one another but also in their own minds.

Only Eloquentia stayed calm and firm. At night, she left the Assembly Hall in loveliness, and each morning returned the same way. Lana's desire to meet her got rather desperate. So she plied Bugbite with an extra-large helping of yeast and begged her to show her the way.

Bugbite wove through the air, one wing stuttering, the other beating triple time and making a wheezing hum. Lana tried to memorize the route: down the stairs to the library, through the stacks, past the desk where the scribes turned in their daily journals, down a spiral staircase to the archives, and up a ladder and through a hatch to the bell ringer's loft.

There, a short, heavy girl with a very sweet face started up from her nap. Ropes hung from the ceiling, draped like curtains to rest on wall hooks. The tails of the ropes were covered with bulging woolen sallies, striped red and white.

"Don't touch!" the girl yelled just as Lana was about to give one of the sallies an experimental tug.

Lana's hand hung in the air.

"Whyever not?"

"You'll break your arm, that's why not. That's if the rope doesn't wrap around your neck and dash you up and down like a puppet." She pointed at the ceiling. "The bass bell weighs three tons. Do you want to be dead?"

"Not yet," Lana said. "Maybe I'll come back in a week or so."

"Maybe I don't know the snake's road too well," Bugbite whispered. It was as close to an apology as Lana had ever heard from a fairy.

"That's fine," Lana said. "Onward!"

Lana gave up trying to memorize the route. Too many false turns, too much backtracking. It took an hour, and when they finally got to the courtyard, the dancer wasn't there. She might have already come and gone, but it didn't matter. The night was warm. Stars glinted overhead.

Lana stood on the blue stone at the courtyard's center and bent forward, letting her head hang, trying to loosen her cramped shoulders. Old scribes stooped, shoulders rounded as if hunched against the cold. Lana was determined to avoid that fate and stretched regularly—or whenever she remembered.

Above, Bugbite's balcony was just a dark splotch in the night. Other windows were more obvious, other balconies less recessed. Putting her foot where the dancer did, moving her body in the space she'd occupied—it all seemed a bit magical. Eloquentia had blessed this courtyard.

Lana spread her arms wide and let her head fall back, admiring the milky spray of stars overhead. She spun awkwardly on the ball of her foot.

"BB, did you know that what you see in the stars shows you who you really are?"

"No, really?" Bugbite gawped at the night sky as if seeing it for the first time.

"Hearts and flowers, that's what I've always seen," Lana said with pride. "It means I'm a true lover. What do you see?"

Bugbite took her time formulating an answer. She pursed her lips and squinted.

"I see stars," she said finally.

"That means you're practical," Lana said. "Either that or it doesn't work on fairies. Which makes sense. You're strange."

"I am." Bugbite nodded, quite serious. "No, wait. We're not. We're the standard by which all other creatures are measured. The rest of you fall sadly short. Except maybe horses. Horses are pretty."

"Humans are pretty."

"Very few. For example, you're not pretty at all."

"I'm handsome." Lana preened. "Look at my cheekbones. Like a fine plowshare."

She drew her hair over her shoulder, gave it a loving stroke, and flipped it back. The fairy laughed. She swooped high and dove at Lana, then dodged at the last moment.

"Nope, sorry, you're hideous," she said, and patted Lana's cheeks, leaving zaps in a line from her cheekbones to dimples. Lana pushed her away.

"Hundreds of girls think you're wrong."

Bugbite dove at Lana again, with more speed this time, and when the fairy's hands met her shoulders, the surge was tremendous. It knocked her breath out. When the fairy shoved her into the shadows, she had no strength to resist. Lana half collapsed against the wall, legs weak, muscles trembling.

"Don't do that," she slurred.

The dancer appeared in the doorway, ghost-pale in her gauzy shift, her hair tucked under a lace-edged matron's cap that suited her not at all. The glory of her hair was meant to flow in glossy curls over her shoulders as she reclined on a luxurious bed—oh! What a thought. Time to introduce herself.

When Lana tried to push herself off the wall, Bugbite hit her again.

"Stay put," she hissed. Her sharp little teeth grazed the skin of her earlobe. Sparks flew along Lana's jaw and through her tongue.

"Buh buh," she said. "S'no nice."

If Eloquentia noticed them, she gave no sign. She appeared pensive. But that was no surprise. No deputy could be easy with Parliament in crisis, the House divided, doom impending, and factions shifting from day to day.

The dancer dropped to the blue center stone as if felled by an arrow.

"Wuh," Lana said.

Eloquentia was hurt—possibly even dead. Lana's every sinew strained to launch herself across the courtyard and gather the dancer in her arms. But she couldn't move; Bugbite had made sure of that. But why? Was death coming so soon for them all?

If so, fine. Lana was valiant enough to welcome death— or so she told herself. And the dancer didn't need help. It was just a pose. A facsimile of death. She gathered her legs beneath her and stretched to greet the moon, reaching high with every muscle until balanced on the ball of one foot. Lana half expected her to lift off and fly.

What followed wasn't one of the wistful, dreamy performances Lana had admired from the balcony. Her movements were angular, agitated, and fast. Arms snapped out like whips, feet cleaved the paving stones, kicking up grime from the margins of the slabs. She orbited the courtyard, gaining speed until the velocity of her dance seemed like it could unhinge Parliament. Lift the whole structure—gates, battlements, houses, and abbey—off the sand and up to the stars.

When she collapsed in another deathlike drop, dust puffed around her crumpled form.

Lana lurched into the courtyard, dodging Bugbite's nasty fingers.

"That was amazing," she said. "Really super fantastic."

The dancer opened one eye.

"When I first saw you dance, I thought you were barely more than a girl. For a woman of your advanced age to dance like this, well, obviously you're a prodigy from birth or something of the sort. Did I say I was impressed? I am. Extremely."

The dancer's chest heaved. Sweat pearled on her brow. Her matronly cap had flown off, and her glorious loose hair spread over the grimy stones.

"You're Eloquentia de la Barre." Lana patted her own chest as if introducing herself.

Ridiculous. It wasn't as if she didn't know how to talk to girls. Sweet talk was her specialty.

This was Bugbite's fault. Rough treatment had turned Lana's tongue to lead. Best keep quiet until she had herself under control. She smiled suavely and put out her hand, offering to help the dancer to her feet, but just a moment too late. Eloquentia rose and settled the folds of her shift around her hips.

"Sorry, Madame la Députée," Bugbite called out from the shadows. "This is what happens when we let scribes out of their cages."

Lana aimed a rude gesture at her friend. Then she put her hands in her pockets and rocked back on one heel. It was a good pose, she knew from experience. Made the most of her enviable jawline.

"Come along, you waster," Bugbite sang out. "It's time you were in bed."

Lana ignored the fairy.

"I didn't mean you were old," she explained. "Just significantly older than I thought you were at first. Of course you're not old. You're younger than my mother, for instance."

"Don't make me come over there, Lana!" Bugbite yelled.

"I'm not worried!" Lana shouted back. She gave Eloquentia a suave smile. "My fairy friend is too shy to come where you can see her. Which is too bad. She's not all that homely. I mean by human standards."

Bugbite groaned.

"Life at Parliament roughens a person's edges," Eloquentia said, and Lana nearly swooned. Fairy words with French vowels, and a deep buckwheat-honey tone.

"Oh my, you have a beautiful voice, too." Lana grinned like a scarecrow, stuffed and brainless, but she couldn't help it. "Why don't you talk more? You could fix Parliament if you'd just open your mouth."

"I could say the same to you, scribe." Eloquentia's wary manner turned frosty. "Why don't you fix Parliament? Or best yet, why doesn't that fairy fix it?" She pointed into the shadows.

"Me?" Bugbite yelped.

"We're not deputies, though," Lana answered.

"You exaggerate the power of a deputy. We are all prisoners here, beating our fists on the walls to get out. That's the way the fairies like it. That's what they designed."

Bugbite screeched. It sounded like a child's cry. She flew from the shadows at sparrow speed, grabbed Lana around the waist, and tried to drag her away.

"She doesn't know what she's talking about, Madame la Députée," Bugbite said. "She's only been here a short time."

"Then she's a victim more than any of us," she said.

"I'm a victim, too," Bugbite said. Pulling on Lana didn't work, so she tried pushing. "I can't leave either."

"But when the ocean washes us away, you won't drown. And you won't mourn the dead, either."

Eloquentia snatched her matron's cap off the paving stones and stalked away.

8

The encounter with the dancer dodged Lana's memory like a dream, edges fading, details disintegrating. The more she thought about Eloquentia, the less she remembered. Which was a relief, actually. It had hardly gone as Lana had planned.

She took her usual place in the front row of the scribes' gallery, put her feet up, and tried to get comfortable, but her body ached. And someone was missing. Raina Estrella.

With all the mushroom-induced hearts and flowers flying around the gallery, it took Lana a little while to locate Raina Estrella sitting in the third row, far corner beside Melodia and Una, who were, as usual, kissing. The scribe caught Lana's eye and shrugged.

Fine, if Raina Estrella's page objected to her love participating in a little innocent and healthful flirtation, Lana would stand down with grace. She gave Raina Estrella a happy wave and a grin. With more room on the bench, she could really stretch out and get comfortable.

"Why did you keep zapping me?" she asked Bugbite when the fairy settled at her now-accustomed spot on the back of the bench, at Lana's shoulder. "Last night, I mean. I still hurt."

Bugbite shrugged. She looked grumpier than usual, honeycomb eyes clouded and gray, whiskers frazzled.

"Deputies don't need to get accosted in the middle of the night by idiot scribes."

"I was perfectly civil." Or, at least, Lana thought so. Maybe her tongue had stumbled, but that was only natural when facing such a beauty. Eloquentia wouldn't have minded. "She liked talking to me. It was you she had a problem with."

"Parliament follows a hierarchy of respect. Someone like you wouldn't understand that, though."

"Okay, teach me. Who's at the top?"

"The Maréchal Assemblay, of course. Then the Speaker." Bugbite nodded at the white-haired great-grandmam reclining in her throne-like chair. "Then the deputies, according to how long they've served. Librarians and pages are about equal. Then the rest of you humans, with scribe wasters at the bottom."

"Aren't you fairies on top?"

Bugbite shivered as if shaking off an annoying insect. She darted to the back row, where Vera, Syrene, and Margit were all napping. She pinched them awake and began hectoring them.

Fairies were on top, obviously. Both literally and organizationally.

Though flashy and gorgeous, the Parliamentary fairies were easy to overlook. The human gaze was attuned to the human form, and the design of the great, old cathedral had been informed by human ideals, to support ancient human ways of thinking. Nothing natural or nature-like about it. But fairies were everywhere. Most of them were tiny, and all were good at hiding. No wonder Bugbite had been relegated to managing scribes. Among the beauties, she'd stand out like a shock.

Nature, perfected, that's what the fairies claimed to be, and nobody had been able to prove them wrong. Their castles and aeries sat lightly on the landscape. Their innovations left no detritus, their industries no spoil pits. They cut no firewood, burned no charcoal, mined no tin, forged no iron, plowed no fields, and yet lived in health and luxury. If they had jewels, they were found among streambed gravel, precut and polished. If they had gold, it was pulled from the stamens of sunflowers and knit into rings and wreaths. If a fairy had fine clothes, who could say she hadn't grown them from her own skin?

When the Speaker began the session, Lana watched with more interest than she had in previous days, paying attention not only to the hallucinogenic patterns that wove through the air (antlered snails this morning, jousting like olden knights). When the visions faded, she began watching the fairies and deputies.

Eloquentia, she couldn't help but notice, arrived late. It earned her a scolding from an infinitesimally small, daffodil-yellow fairy dressed in a wisp of pearly gauze. The dancer replied with a respectful inclination of her head. Was that all the Parliamentary fairies did, ride roughshod over the deputies?

"You could just let us all go, you know," she said to Bug-bite when the fairy returned to her side later in the afternoon. The deputy from Weigh-North-Yorking had been orating for an hour about wool exports and salt-cod tariffs, keeping Lana dashing along the page to record her words. "My fingers are sore from all this writing, and why? It's not like any of this matters."

"This is your government, not mine." Bugbite was clearly nursing one of her cranky moods. Lana reached into her pocket. Was there any reason they shouldn't take solace a little early? It had been a hard day. Maybe a grain each, just to get them through the session?

The yeast brightened the fairy's mood. When a Magyar deputy took the floor and began orating in her own language, Lana could put her pen down without risking a lecture.

"What do you mean it's not your government?" Lana asked. "Look at all the fairies down there. What would happen if all the deputies just walked out?"

"Nothing you'd appreciate."

"Their fairies would chase them down and force them back into session. You have us on the point of a sword. Government by hostage. Is that the fairy way?"

Bugbite sighed. "Let's take another grain."

Lana was happy to oblige and even happier when, a little later, a movement down on the floor caught her eye. It was Eloquentia. She twisted in her chair, gazing right up at them.

"Look," Lana whispered. She nudged her friend's hip with her elbow. "Go say hello."

"No," Bugbite said, horrified.

"Then tell her hello from me. Come on, what are wings for?"

Bugbite picked at a thread on her ragged bodice. Fine. If the fairy was too cowardly to take advantage of the moment, Lana wasn't.

She loosened her shoulders and laid her arm along the back of the bench. Eloquentia was a woman of taste. She'd appreciate a view of Lana's three-quarter profile, her excellent chin and dark brows. She raised her pen as if ready to write down a thought and let her eyes drift to meet Eloquentia's. Lana gave the dancer her most charming smile and lowered her pen.

"You and I were just talking about something very important," she told Bugbite, not taking her eyes off the enchanting woman half-turned in her seat below. "But suddenly, nothing is more important than her."

"You talk nonsense to hear the sound of your own voice," Bugbite replied.

Lana tapped the tail of her pen on her lower lip.

"That is a very fair criticism."

Eventually, Eloquentia looked away. Lana couldn't tell if she'd liked what she'd seen or had simply been allowing her eyes to rest on a semi-agreeable object while thinking of other things. She didn't look up again, and when the night ended, she paced across the Assembly Hall, silent and pensive, surrounded by a gaggle of arguing deputies, and passed through the grand doorway without looking back.

Eloquentia's exit wasn't enough to put Lana in a mood—nothing she liked better than a love chase—but the scribes' supper was a sad state of affairs and the scribes themselves even sadder. Seven drab, ink-stained young women, all staring at the congealed innards of their pies as if the future could be scried there. Lana looked from face to doleful face.

"The cooks left the salt out of the pies and let them sit for half a day. That's nothing to cry over."

"Don't you pay attention to anything?" Raina Estrella only raised her voice slightly, but it was uncharacteristic enough to make all the other scribes raise their heads.

"Considering how woeful you all look, I'm fairly glad I didn't." Lana scooped the last bit of gummy paste from her pie and waved her spoon. Stringy scraps of duck dangled like octopus legs. "Things aren't quite as bad as all that."

She said it to cheer them up, but also because she believed it in her heart. In no imaginable world would a woman like Eloquentia—talented, sensitive, intelligent—allow anything bad to happen. It was easier to imagine a mother leaving her children to starve on the streets.

The scribes just shook their heads. Raina Estrella looked thoughtful for a moment, then frowned.

"You're new here." She returned her attention to picking at her pie with the edge of her spoon.

Bugbite dropped from the rafters, where she'd been sucking the pollen from the stamens of a giant lily.

"I think it's time," the fairy said in Lana's ear. She shivered her wings, shedding scales onto the floor, and buzzed out the window.

Lana shared out yeast to each scribe, generously and with no stinting. When each pen was nearly empty, she scooped a few flecks of piecrust into the barrel and added a sweet crystal from the rim of the scribes' honeypot. She shook the mixtures vigorously and put the pens back in her pocket, where, against the warmth of her body, the yeast would bloom and multiply.

Within moments, the tense atmosphere relaxed. Melodia and Una rolled right into bed and drew the curtains shut. Syrene began shuffling cards while Margit and Vera set up the pegs on their betting board.

"I finally understand why you smell so good." Raina

Estrella leaned over the table, chin in both hands. "And how you managed to charm our horrid little beast."

"I don't think that's a fair—"

Raina Estrella stood and waved both arms at the doorway, where her page stood, feet planted, arms crossed.

"We weren't flirting!" she yelled. "Come over here. I want to show you something." She climbed over the table and dropped to the bench at Lana's side. "Come. Here." She smacked her palm on the tabletop.

The page crossed the scribes' hall with carefully contained dignity. Raina Estrella pointed at Lana's neck, right under the ear.

"Smell her."

Lana scrambled away. Under normal circumstances, she wasn't at all adverse to a threesome. It had been days and days since Lana had indulged herself in a night of love. Taking two to bed might make up for lost time, but prior experience showed that getting between a fractious couple, even in the most delightful of circumstances, tended to bring regrets on all sides. Still, she might not get another chance . . .

Lana caught herself just in time. She declined, shaking her head and smiling sheepishly. Where was Bugbite? What were friends if you couldn't count on them to rescue you from awkward propositions?

To cover her embarrassment, Lana made a show of brushing crumbs from her clothes. She checked her pens, rebuttoned her vest, and straightened the tails of her coat. By the time she was done, Raina Estrella and her page were in full clinch and sinking toward the floor. Lana coughed, pretended to pick a bit of fluff from her cuff, and wandered out of the hall.

"You really don't want to leave me on my own," Lana said. Her voice echoed as she descended to the library. "There's no telling what kind of trouble I could get into."

The library was nearly empty. No fairies anywhere, but a trio of bookworms were snuggled into the leather chairs around the hearth, nose-deep in thick novels. Lana joined them, scanned a few pages from a pile of discarded volumes while she pondered her options.

She would certainly be able to find the courtyard, sooner or later, using the standard hedge-maze method of following the right wall and not varying. But she wanted to avoid running into anyone from the kitchens. Judging from the state of the pies, the cooks were foul and fomenting revolution.

In situations like these, a woman with a demanding temperament might work hard to solve her problem. But luck had always been Lana's friend. She set off down an unpromising corridor—narrow, low, but well-trod—and trusted that luck would bring her face-to-face with Eloquentia. And when luck smiled, what delights might follow? Perhaps a tryst in an Assembly Hall nook, spiced with the near possibility of death and the nearer possibility of being discovered. Lana would cherish the opportunity to nuzzle the skin under Eloquentia's ear, breathe her warm scent, glide fingertips over wrists, collarbones, nape. And kisses—the lightest of affectionate touches deepening to something more. Everything more.

It would happen. Surely after weeks of unproductive, vexing Parliamentary sessions, Eloquentia would be desperate for distraction.

These thoughts begged the question: What could Lana call her? *Madam Deputy* or *Madame la Députée* would be correct, but she couldn't quite stomach using cold honorifics with a woman with whom she shared such passionate, if wholly imaginary intimacy.

Following the right-wall principle, Lana found herself at the end of a series of derelict rooms, with only her own footprints in the dust for company. But it wasn't quite a dead end. In the corner was a narrow slot, just wide enough to pass through, though she had to duck her head to fit. The spiral passage beyond was a tight fit and dark, too, with narrow steps she could just navigate by reaching ahead and feeling carefully with her toes.

As she climbed, the night air took on a seaweed-and-saltwater bite. Just as she was becoming winded, the passage opened into a tower room. Arrow slits threw rectangles of moonlight across the mossy floor, illuminating a ladder scaly with rust. The trapdoor above had long since rotted away. Lana had her feet on a forward footing, so why not give it a climb?

Why not, indeed? And it paid off, for the view from the tower was incomparable, with ancient gap-toothed battlements giving way to steep, rain-shedding slate roofs. Beyond, a low tide exposed misty flats, the sands laced with moonlit ribbons of tidal creeks. But the best view was closer at hand—under her very fingers, in fact, for the tower's ancient stones sprouted with mushrooms.

"Hey, now," Lana said. "So this is where you hide them."

Lana's greedy fingers hovered over a large, meaty mushroom. But she wasn't silly enough to pluck strange fungus under moonlight, not quite. One type of mushroom looked very like another. Lana knew the difference between choux and puff pastry, but mushrooms were mysterious even by daylight.

She blew the mushrooms a kiss goodbye and had just set her boot on the ladder when movement over a distant rooftop caught her eye. Fairies. Lots of them. Some sat on the peaks of roofs and chimneys, some hovered low, others flitted through windows or dropped down from the high mist. Bugbite was the easiest individual to track. Her garish stripes stood out even in moonlight. She kept well back from the others. With her stiff, jaw-out stance, she looked distinctively belligerent compared to her nimble little compatriots.

Lana crouched low and watched. Fairies flew in from oceanward, each pair carrying a fairy-size treasure chest between them. They set the chests on a flat rooftop and began distributing the contents. One per fairy, larger items to the larger fairies, smaller to the smaller, but all the same shape: a rod or tube with a grip on the end. The fairies brandished them at one another, arms extended, sighting down the barrels and tittering.

One tiny fairy, after being aimed at by her companion, thrust herself backward in the air and allowed herself to fall, arms and legs limp. She caught herself inches from the ground and sped back to rejoin the game.

Bugbite didn't play. She didn't laugh. She tucked the rod in the band of her petticoat and watched. She'd folded her arms so tightly, it looked like she was hugging herself. Angry, obviously. Lana felt she knew the little beauty well enough by now and could guess why. She was excluding herself from the game because past experience had proven she wasn't welcome.

"Oh, BB," Lana whispered. "That's got to sting."

Some people believed fairies were better than humans.

Wiser and more just, if always horridly grumpy. But Lana believed that anything humans did had its fairy equivalent. Humans excluded the awkward, the homely, the deformed and decrepit. Though wrong, it was human nature. So it followed that fairies would do the same.

Lana's heart hurt to see her friend so shunned. If she could fly, she'd launch herself over the roofs and play mother. She'd scold the fairies up one side and down the other and give them a few things to think about.

As it was, all she could do was watch as the fog descended, wrapping the world in layers of wool. She listened to fog-muffled fairy laughter until the cold entered her bones and chased her indoors.

9

Bugbite woke the scribes with bruising pinches, and Lana was not spared.

"That's not nice," she complained, and when Bugbite pinched her again, she grabbed the fairy's wrists and yanked her through the curtains. The fairy fell against her. Velvety wings batted Lana's face. A hard object banged against Lana's hip.

"Aw, how sweet," Lana said. "You brought a toy."

"I didn't—" the fairy sputtered, struggling. "I wouldn't—"

"Oh, you would so."

She shifted her grip so the fairy's wrists were trapped in one fist and made a grab for the object. Bugbite writhed. She threw herself out of the alcove, dragging Lana behind her. When they hit the floor, there was no mistaking the clang of metal on wood.

"Let go!" the fairy screamed, truly terrified.

When Lana released her, Bugbite scrambled along the floor on all fours, spiderlike, until her wings found purchase on air. She darted to a high corner and brandished the metal tube. She aimed it at Lana, at the other scribes, and back at Lana again. Her eyes were gray and wide with terror.

"Don't you ever, ever do that again!" she shrieked.

"I was just roughhousing." Lana stood and brushed herself off. "It was only a bit of fun."

"That is not how you have fun," the fairy screeched. "You hurt me."

"If so, I'm not sorry. You hurt us all the time. I'm tired of it. I have bruises. We all do. You need to stop it or else."

"Or else what?" The fairy stared right down the barrel at Lana. The tip of the object was shaking—Bugbite's hands were shaking. Lana had really spooked her.

"Stop pointing that thing at me. It's making me nervous. What is it anyway? Some kind of gun?"

"Or else what?" Bugbite yelled.

Lana spread her hands wide.

"Or else nothing. If you don't pinch me, I won't grab you. Deal?"

Bugbite fled. She didn't appear again until the scribes were on their way to the gallery. The fairy flew behind them as they shuffled through the halls. The gun bounced on her hip.

Lana raised her voice.

"In my mother's house, when someone apologizes, that's the end of the dispute. Continuing to be offended is bad form."

"But you didn't apologize," said Raina Estrella.

"No, and neither did she."

The Assembly Hall was in disarray. No dignity, no pomp, just a couple hundred deputies mobbing the Speaker's throne. And fairies—many more than usual, all carrying guns.

Lana sat alone on the front bench. It didn't look like the session would be beginning anytime soon, so she stretched out full length and settled in for a peaceful doze. She couldn't quite get comfortable, though. Something kept jolting her awake. A twinge in her ankle, a nip on her elbow, an itch on the tip of her nose, her eyebrow, her lip.

She squinted through her eyelashes, and sure enough, Bugbite was up in the rafters, aiming the gun at her. An insistent itch bloomed on Lana's earlobe. But no, she wouldn't scratch it, wouldn't give the fairy the satisfaction. She'd lie still and prove that no matter what torture she applied, Lana was above it. Impervious. Serene.

But after a few minutes, she was writhing, scratching furiously.

"I'm sorry!" she shouted to the rafters. "I would never, ever hurt you. If you don't know that by now, you're irretrievably stupid. Okay?"

"That is not an apology, Lana," Raina Estrella shouted from the other end of the gallery.

But it seemed good enough for Bugbite. She put the gun down. Soon enough, she was back in her place at Lana's shoulder.

"You're a human, and that means you're scary," the fairy said. "Humans hurt fairies, you know."

"That was a long time ago."

"Not for us." Bugbite's wings drooped. Flakes rained off them, dusting the bench with acid-yellow glitter. Lana took her friend's little hand in her own.

"I'm sorry I frightened you," she said. "I won't do it again."

The fairy nodded. She reached into her pocket. Lana brightened, sure her friend was about to produce a mushroom, offer her a scale or two. But the fairy had second thoughts and withdrew her hand empty. Instead, she patted the gun.

"Can I see it?" Lana asked.

Bugbite hesitated a moment, then slid the tube off her hip. A handle pierced with tiny holes was appended to the barrel, which had a V-shaped sight on the handle end and a small prong on the tip. Bugbite gripped the handle, covering the holes with her fingers and palm. Since she was such a large fairy, the handle was too small for her. In her grip, it looked like a child's toy.

"There's nothing to it. A flute is more complicated." Bugbite pointed it at the floor and sighted along the barrel. "Anything I can do with my hands, this allows me to do at range. Most fairies hold it to their mouths and spit to shoot a projectile, but that's not my talent. It's quite miraculous, really."

"BB," Lana replied, very serious. "It's not miraculous, it's malicious. What has anyone here done to you?"

"It's not about what you have done. It's about what you can do. What you will do, if fairykin doesn't take care. It's about keeping you humans to your agreements and making Parliament work."

"Who cares if it works? What does it even matter? I can tell you nobody in London cares what Parliament does."

"You would care very much if all of Europe went to war each spring, like you used to."

"There's nothing bad about war. It's normal human behavior."

"That's the most ignorant thing I've ever heard." Bugbite drew back, disgusted.

"Anyway, we haven't had a war for so long, I doubt we'd

even remember how to go about it. What are the fairies so scared of?"

"You!" the fairy yelled. "We're scared of you, okay? If wars were just you killing each other, that would be fine. But you kill us, too, and everything else. You burn forests and salt fields. You turn meadows into graveyards and trails into miles-wide paths of destruction. And when we try to keep you out of our aeries and castles, you break in and kill us all. Or worse."

"No, that can't be right." It wasn't the stories of war Lana had heard, with sisterhoods of valiant knights traveling the land, fighting for justice.

Bugbite reached out, clearly preparing to jab her finger into Lana's flesh and jolt her eyes loose from her skull. Lana recoiled. Bugbite crossed her arms tightly, jabbing the air with her finger like a frustrated tutor, punctuating her point.

"All you need to do is send your deputies to Parliament and talk out your differences in a reasonable manner. Make treaties and trade agreements, negotiate border disputes, and do whatever else you think is so important. If you can't do these very simple, basic things, we'll drown you and start over. Don't think we won't."

Lana made an effort to stretch her arms across the back of the bench and relax her posture. Anger was never going to be any use here.

"I heard you fairies used to be happy creatures, once upon a time. Now you just boss us around."

"We can't help it. Dealing with humans puts us in a bad mood."

"My mother says that every time she gets called to the

front of the shop. You're right. Humans are the worst." Lana laughed.

"Some of you are okay."

Lana felt a surge of warm affection, despite the gun on her friend's hip. Bugbite had used the weapon to torment her and could, Lana suspected, cripple her with it anytime she chose. Still, it was not much different from her sisters, who could— and did—wound one another daily with fanged words, barbed opinions, and poisonous ideas. Lana put an affection- ate arm around Bugbite's hips and drew her close.

Over the Speaker's throne, a tiny purple fairy brandished her silver gun, like an evil-tempered carter lashing her whip. Lana couldn't tell if she was actually zapping people or just threatening to. But her rage was so intense, it made the worst of Bugbite's tantrums look calm.

The Speaker sat abruptly and banged her gavel, calling the session to order even before the deputies had found their seats. She gave a long speech about the solemnity of Parlia- mentary proceedings, the oaths each deputy was bound to uphold, the sacred trust their precincts had placed in them, and so on, at length, with great gravitas and many noble ges- tures. So far so good. Then it all fell apart, because what the Speaker proposed, eventually, after much careful cushioning, was for Parliament to abandon its two and a half centuries of adherence to a strict majority of two-thirds and adopt a rule of simple majority for votes.

Horror. Deputies pounded tables and gnashed their teeth. Glitter rained from the wings of the fairies overhead, flecking the deputies' purple robes with all the colors of spring as they waved their arms and demanded to be recognized by the Speaker.

If what was going on down on the floor made any sense at all, Lana might have wished she'd paid more attention to her tutor's governance lectures. As it was, she very much doubted being a book-nosed student would have made any difference.

When Berkingmiddleshire claimed priority over the floor, Lana had paid enough attention to the deputy's past speeches to predict what she would say—copper mines, iron trade, tin tariffs, overland and coastal shipping, and other heavy subjects. But she didn't. Oh, certainly, she began talking about rocks, but only as a foundation for Angland's ancient history, waxing at length about its ochre-stained burial mounds, standing stone complexes, and hilltop fortifications, and about how they proved Angland was far more special than any other land. Even if others had similar relics, she claimed, they were all pallid copies.

Worst luck, the Berkingmiddleshire deputy never spoke anything but Anglish, so recording her every word was Lana's job. In the meantime, the other scribes napped. Deputies chatted with their neighbors or scribbled letters. Pages gathered in little gangs, leaned against the walls, stretched, scratched, and gossiped. Fairies buzzed around, pretty as butterflies. What sense they were making of Berkingmiddleshire's finest, Lana couldn't tell.

Eloquentia kept to her seat, serene and relaxed, but if her expression ever betrayed any annoyance, Lana couldn't see it. She kept her back turned to the scribes' gallery.

Three hours in, and Berkingmiddleshire was still on her feet, talking loudly as ever, though in her patriotic fervor, she'd knocked the pins loose from her helmetlike hair. Hanks of iron-gray hung down her neck like a neighborhood frowze. She fidgeted, dancing from foot to foot in slow time.

"This is torture," Lana said. "Is the Speaker going to let her go on forever?"

"Protocol says she can speechify for as long as she can stay on her feet," said Raina Estrella.

Lana's fellow scribes had moved into the first and second rows, lending Lana some moral support.

"If she can stay upright and keep talking, she doesn't have to yield the floor," said Margit. "Maybe she'll collapse."

"Maybe her bladder will burst," said Syrene.

"She's not going to make it that long," Lana said. "I'm not going to make it that long, and I'm a third of her age and sitting down."

But unlike Lana, the deputy was offered the occasional break. Her cronies from Surreysex and Devon-Longlizard gave comments disguised as questions, waxing at length about Anglish potency, and giving Berkingmiddleshire the chance to rest her voice.

"She's going to fall over," Raina Estrella said. "This is nearly done. Hang on to your pen."

"Like I have any choice," Lana grumbled. Her fingers were permanently clawed. Only pride kept Lana from letting the pages devolve into nonsense squiggles.

But the deputy didn't fall, and she didn't shut up. Lana kept at it for as long as she could, then dropped her pen and lunged for the pot cupboard at the back of the gallery.

"As long as that idiot can keep talking, I can keep scribing," she told Bugbite, who was hovering over her protectively. "I just didn't want to soil the bench."

She tried her pen in her left hand. Years back, to impress girls, she'd tried learning ambi-hand, but hadn't kept it up. Turned out, few girls were impressed by scribe tricks.

"Take it in turns," Bugbite told the other scribes. "Just write what you hear. Doesn't matter if it's right. At this point, I doubt anyone knows the difference between gibberish and Anglish nonsense."

"I can do this," Lana insisted.

"Why, though?" Bugbite patted Lana's shoulder fondly.

They retreated to the back of the gallery. Discreetly, Bugbite peeled a couple of scales off a mushroom.

"She must be wearing a diaper," Lana observed. Bugbite giggled.

Toward the end of the session, Lana finally got a look at Eloquentia's face. She stood and gazed into the scribes' gallery, lips pale, expression serious. Lana held her breath and tried to look noble.

"Do you see that?" she whispered in Bugbite's ear. "She's thinking about me."

The fairy's little face soured.

"It's just the mushroom making hearts and flowers out of nothing," Bugbite said. "I see them, too."

Lana moved to the front row, but instead of sitting in her accustomed spot, she put both hands on the rail and leaned out as if searching for something. Bugbite hovered at her shoulder.

"What are you looking for?" the fairy whispered.

"Nothing. I want her to see me in the best light."

"Oh, I get it. You're posing." Bugbite swept Lana's lapels, straightened her collar. "You're a little rumpled."

Lana was certain her tableau was composed for maximum effect. And indeed, the deputy did look enraptured. Tiny birds haloed her dark head and sang songs of love. Or at least, that's what Lana saw. When the mushroom haze dissolved, the deputy's expression was more serious than ever.

"She's still looking at us," Bugbite hissed through clenched teeth.

Eloquentia pointed at the sky and brought her palms together. Then she made a square with her thumbs and forefingers.

"She wants something from us."

Lana couldn't think what. The tweeting birds were back, filling the Assembly Hall with song.

A shade of impatience passed over Eloquentia's face. She repeated the gestures, slower, and then made a little turn that set her skirts swirling.

"The courtyard tonight," Lana and Bugbite said in unison.

Lana brought her palm to her chest in an elegant gesture and mouthed the word *Me?* with all the fake humility she could muster. It was the only honorable reaction to being propositioned at a distance.

The deputy pointed at Lana and at Bugbite, and then, as if to ensure they understood her meaning, held up two fingers.

Lana inclined her head graciously.

An assignation, what could be more exciting? Well, not having Bugbite included in the invitation, that would be better. Having enough time for a bath, that would be good, too.

When Berkingmiddleshire finally sat, the Speaker's call for further comments was met by groans, waving fists, and vague threats against anyone who dared take the floor. The vote was called, and tired as the deputies were, they all ran to join the Nays. No formal count was required to validate the strict majority—the first non-hung vote of the year.

Lana searched for Eloquentia in the mass of celebrating deputies, dreading to see her in a clinch with some handsome colleague from Budapest or Athens. But she wasn't. Her seat was on the side of Nay, and she'd stayed there, her slender shoulders high and stiff with tension as if waiting for a blow.

10

Eloquentia was late.

"Did I imagine it?" Lana asked her fairy friend.

"You imagine lots of things."

The shirt Lana had changed into was clean and fresh, but not her best. Ink dotted its ruffled cuffs. Lana tucked them into the sleeves of her tailcoat, then thought the better of it. She took off her coat and draped it over her shoulders, then rolled up her sleeves to better display her attractive forearms. She pulled her hair loose and rumpled it to achieve a just-rolled-out-of-bed effect.

"How do I look?"

"You've got mossy teeth." Bugbite was in a mood, but she wasn't wrong. Lana had grabbed a stem of mint from one of the kitchen's windowsill pots and chewed it to freshen her breath. The pulped mint caked Lana's mouth, and she had nothing to rinse with. She spat into her handkerchief and swabbed her teeth as best she could. But that was a mistake, too. If Eloquentia became teary, she would have nothing to offer, no returning-your-handkerchief excuse for another meeting.

A rookie mistake. She ought to know enough to carry two handkerchiefs. One for common use, one for seductions.

But now: footsteps. Eloquentia appeared, cloaked in

midnight-blue folds, her lovely face shaded under a hood.

Lana staggered as if bowled over by the sight of the dancer crossing the courtyard.

"Where is the fairy?" Eloquentia said. Hardly the proper form for such a meeting, but perhaps they did things differently in her part of France.

"Shy in the face of your beauty," Lana began, voice low, "she has drawn back into the shadows. As I myself—"

"Where?" Eloquentia squinted into the courtyard's shadows. "Ah," she said. "Come out. Join us."

Bugbite yelped. The dancer crossed her hands over her breast.

"S'il vous plaît?"

Slowly, Bugbite crossed the courtyard. She hovered just behind Lana's shoulder as if for protection.

"You two seem friendly. What do you call yourselves?"

"I am Lana, Lana Baker, and this is Beauty Bugbite."

"I meant, what are you to each other?"

"We're friends," said Lana. "Fast friends forever, right, BB?"

The fairy nodded vigorously.

"That's rare," said Eloquentia.

"Not rare in your experience, I'm certain." Lana returned to her slow, seductive tone. "A woman like you must make friends wherever—"

"No, I mean friendship between human and fairy is rare. Not unheard of, but conditions mostly don't allow it."

"Conditions?" Lana asked.

"Let's not waste time with generalities. Tell me about yourselves."

Lana was glad to answer.

"I came to Parliament a few weeks ago, homesick, and missing my mother and sisters most desperately." That was a massive exaggeration, but if Eloquentia wanted to take the upper hand, Lana was not above playing the ingénue. "When Bugbite and I watched you dance, my heart healed."

"You've only known each other a brief time? I was mistaken, then. Good night." She walked away.

"Wait," Lana called softly. "The length of a friendship is no proof of its strength. Bugbite and I have been tried and tested, have we not, BB?"

"Just this morning, in fact," Bugbite said.

"Ours is a true, loving friendship," Lana insisted.

"Is it indeed?" Eloquentia rubbed her chin between thumb and forefinger. "Tell me, Beauty Bugbite, how will you feel when Lana Baker drowns?"

Bugbite stared. Her jaw worked, lips opening and closing. No sound came out.

When Eloquentia drew the cloak around her, she seemed to grow taller.

"I don't expect you care about me or the other deputies. But when your friend dies, will you feel anything? Tell me. Will your love drown with her?"

Bugbite's mouth gaped wide. Her eyes turned gray in the moonlight.

"Should I tell you what I think?" the deputy asked. "I think you will rise the next day, perfectly contented. You'll lick the dew from the flowers and never think of Lana Baker again. Am I right?"

"I don't think that's a fair question," said Lana. This was hardly the way she'd expected the encounter to progress.

"Since you and I are going to drown, I believe it's very fair."

"Hey, now," Lana said, dropping all pretense of seduction. "Tonight's vote went well."

Eloquentia laughed. "Do you think so? But you're new here. Come and sit with me while Beauty Bugbite thinks."

She led Lana to a pair of benches in a shadow under the courtyard wall.

"I have more unfair questions, but this one is for you."

"A lady may ask anything of me."

That was good. Lana hadn't been knocked so far off-kilter that gallant phrases were beyond her reach. If only she could just get her composure back. She draped her tailcoat over her shoulders, then crossed her legs and leaned back on one hand, striking a pose that looked both unaffected and romantic—or so she hoped. But the dancer's thoughts were far away.

"Why do the Anglish court death?" she asked.

Lana's coat threatened to slide from her shoulders.

"We don't," she said hastily, and then regretted it. Contradicting a lady was hardly the route to kisses. "Except when we do. I mean, everyone does, sometimes, don't they?"

She hoped Bugbite would rescue her, but the fairy was still gobsmacked. She hovered in the middle of the courtyard, rotating slowly as if looking for a way out. No, Lana was on her own. She'd have to go on the offensive.

"If I were to ask you why the French are so blunt, would you be able to answer?" she asked.

"Certainly. It's because the stupidity of others is extremely irritating."

"I understand. Living among mortals must test your patience."

The smallest possible unit of amusement crossed Eloquentia's face. It gave Lana courage to continue.

"If I must express an opinion, with all humility and truthfulness, I would say we Anglish are belligerent by nature. If we're not quarreling with our neighbors, we feel we might cease to exist."

"That's ridiculous."

Lana leaned close.

"Very likely. But you asked, and I find myself unable to deny you anything."

The compliment missed the mark. The deputy was obviously chewing over a problem. Still, compliments and gallant statements were the only script Lana knew. They'd rarely failed her before. She'd just keep at it and see what happened.

"The Anglish are blessed." Eloquentia spoke slowly, her tone plummy and persuasive. "Your babies are fat, your cream is rich, and the grain ripens in autumn. You have good soil, plenty of rain, and all the fish you can catch. What do you have to quarrel over?"

"You don't need to convince me, Madam Deputy. Angland is everything you say. Though in my opinion, the most benevolent, most desirable land is wherever you lay your feet."

She turned toward Lana and looked her square in the face.

"This is not the time or the place," she said.

"Love obeys no restrictions."

Eloquentia grimaced, and even in a fit of desperate courtship, Lana had to admit the expression detracted from her loveliness.

"I'm not here to play courting games," she said. "I'm trying to have an actual conversation."

"Are we not conversing?"

"With both of you," she pleaded. "Beauty Bugbite, please come and talk to me."

Slowly, and with the utmost reluctance possible for a flying creature, Bugbite returned to her spot at Lana's shoulder.

"Why are you being so weird?" Lana whispered in her friend's ear.

"I think we should leave," the fairy whispered back.

Bugbite pointed across the courtyard, where a shadowed form huddled in a doorway. It didn't seem human at first—too lumpy, too awkward. As it moved into the light, it became apparent that it was indeed a person, shuffling backward, stooped over one end of a heavy chest.

Two people carried the other end of the chest. All three were out of breath, nearly gasping, but clearly trying to be quiet. Otherwise, why wouldn't they put their burden down and push or drag it?

"Perhaps this is a common scene at Parliament?" Lana breathed.

It was an excuse to move closer to Eloquentia, catch a whiff of her scent. Powdery and floral, lavender perhaps, or some other herb the French used to keep the vermin from their clothing. Not a strong scent, but with all the romantic ideas spinning in Lana's head, it didn't take much to ignite her imagination with thoughts of getting closer to her warmth.

"Go find out what they're doing," Eloquentia whispered. "Be subtle."

Lana scooped up her jacket, flung it over her shoulder with one finger, and sauntered across the courtyard in her best jolly-neighbor fashion.

"Hey ho, friends," she called. "What you got? Sweets or meats?"

"Go away," said the lead hauler. It was the blond cook who'd given Lana the knife.

"Looks heavy. Can I help?"

"I said get gone," the blond girl snarled. These girls weren't being friendly at all. "Find your own business elsewhere."

"It's no trouble at all." Lana hooked her hands under one of the chest's corners.

"Get off!" The blond girl tried to stomp Lana's foot, but it was a move Lana knew well. She and her sisters had grown up shifting loads from miller's cart to storeroom. The work had also made her a good judge of weight, and the trunk was heavy for its size.

"What's in here?" she asked. "Cream cheeses? Are you making cakes? Do we get a treat tomorrow?"

As if anyone would haul cheese in a chest, but honestly, it was heavy as if filled with water.

The blond girl checked Lana with her hip, putting all her weight behind it. Lana staggered but kept her grip. She laughed, making the courtyard ring.

"You kitchen girls play rough, don't you? And I know why. You need to keep us dancing or there'll be a crowd at your window all day and all night, looking for treats and kisses, and kisses that taste like treats."

The jolly approach definitely wasn't working. Lana had tried her best. Now it was time for something more direct. She gathered her strength, flexed her knees, and lifted. The trunk wavered and toppled, falling to the stones with a massive crunch.

"I told you to fuck off," the blond girl said.

Her fist shot out and clipped Lana's jaw. The hit was solid enough to twist her neck farther than natural. Lana fell to her knees. She tongued a tooth. It waggled in her jaw. Warm blood spurted down her throat. She dropped to her elbows, gagged once, and passed out.

11

Even with her eyes closed, Lana could tell she was in a boudoir. Soft bed, fine linen, feathers above and below as if she were the filling in a layer cake. If she lay there long enough, perhaps a lovely woman would put a soft hand on her brow.

Lana waited, and hoped, but nobody came, not a footfall. Her jaw ached. Her tongue tasted like blood and dirt.

She struggled to loosen the sheets and quilts that entombed her, kicking her legs and yanking at them with her fists. When her arms were free, she felt for her pens. Yes, still safe in her breast pocket.

"Wake up," Bugbite pleaded. "Please, wake up."

It took Lana a moment to remember how to work her eyelids. And when she did, she wished she hadn't. No boudoir, no bed, no lovely lap to cushion her head. Just rock under her and stars overhead. And Bugbite at her side, fists clenched under her pointy little chin, whiskers quivering, eyebrows steeply tented.

Lana pushed herself up and was immediately bowled over again. Bugbite knocked the wind out of her with a desperate embrace.

"Hey, now." Lana patted her friend's back. "A little fracas is nothing to get upset over."

"I thought you were dead and gone. I was going to have to bury you." She put her hands on Lana's cheeks and pressed them together like Lana's face was a waffle and she the iron. "Don't die, please," she said with utmost sincerity.

"I won't," Lana promised.

She disentangled herself from the fairy's embrace and tested her tooth with the tip of her tongue. Loose, but it would probably re-root. And if it didn't, it was lost in Eloquentia's service, so that was fine.

But where was the dancer? Lana and Bugbite were alone, the courtyard empty. The fairy's shed scales reflected moonlight, turning the world glittery and magical, except for one essential missing element.

This was not going according to the courtly script. Take a punch at a lady's request and she leaves before you regain consciousness? Impossible.

"Where's Eloquentia?" The name tripped off Lana's tongue, but she didn't have the right to use it—not yet. "Madam Deputy, I mean. Did she run to fetch help?"

"No, she just left. She said she had to go."

"While I was dying?" Lana was aghast.

"That's what I thought, too, but she said you were fine and would wake up soon." Bugbite squeezed Lana's shoulders. "And you did, so she was right."

Lana pushed the fairy away gently. She reached inside her mouth with two fingers and pressed her loose tooth hard down into her jaw. She wasn't about to lose a tooth for someone who'd trot off as Lana's life was leaking away, no matter how lovely she was.

They trudged back to the scribes' hall, which looked like it, too, had hosted a brawl. All the scribes were in bed—if not their own, then someone else's. Oddly matched feet and legs poked out from the curtains. Lana squeezed Raina Estrella's toe as she passed. The scribe lifted the curtain and looked around, bleary. Her page lover appeared, too, short hair sticking up in spikes.

"Where've you two been?" Raina Estrella whispered.

"Fighting for right," Lana said, and fell into her own bed, behind her own curtains, alone.

~

It's fair to say that Lana had never worked hard to understand anything before.

Why should she? Life was good. Girls were pretty, ale tasty, and work light. Maybe she didn't make her family's life any easier, but she didn't make it much harder, and any problems she caused were leavened by her bright smile and cheery temper. When others caused trouble, they doubled it with grumbling and grudges. Not Lana.

But she was far from home now. Strife was all around, and none of it Lana's doing. But if the problems weren't hers to solve, did that mean she shouldn't try?

In the morning, Lana's face was purple. She swallowed her porridge without chewing, washed up at the scribes' buckets, and went looking for clean underwear. Dug all the way to the bottom of her cupboard, but there was nothing. The mountain of soiled clothes she'd built on the floor hadn't moved.

"What do you think all this is?" Raina Estrella pointed to the clothes strung between the rafters and hanging like flags.

"The laundry maids are refusing to work. Hadn't you noticed?"

"If they can get away with that, why can't we?"

"We could try, if we wanted to risk an early drowning."

"I suppose the fairies don't care if our laundry gets done. Is that right, BB?" Lana called up to the rafters, where Bugbite was sucking the pollen from a huge pink lily.

"If humans want to be filthy, that's your own business," she said.

Lana scrubbed and wrung out a pair of knickers. She put them on wet and struggled to slip her breeches over top. Now her bottom half was just as uncomfortable as the upper: gums tender, jaw stiff, cheek swollen, shoulder complaining. All she needed to complete the misery was a broken toe.

On the way up to the scribes' gallery, Bugbite offered her two mushroom scales.

"I can't do anything about your stupid injuries," she said, "but I can make the day a little less terrible."

Lana put the scales in her pocket. She was trying to think, and the mushroom wouldn't help.

Trying. Thinking. Two unfamiliar concepts. But in all her time sitting above Parliament, writing down everything she heard, Lana couldn't point to much evidence of thinking among the deputies, either. Trying, yes, plenty of that, but trying for what? What were the Anglish deputies trying to accomplish? And in service of what?

Noises of shock and consternation filtered up from the Assembly Hall as the scribes filed into the gallery. No need to search for a cause. Two walls were scarred with graffiti slogans, in letters five feet tall and crusted with fairy glitter:

KEEP HUMANS PASTORAL
SUPPORT FAIRY HEGEMONY
FAIRIES RULE FOREVER

"BB," Lana said. The fairy's eyes were unfocused. Eventually, she located Lana and gave her a vague smile.

"What happened here, BB?" Lana asked.

She had to repeat the question several times and point down at the walls. The fairy glanced at the slogans, then tracked something along the ceiling, like a cat with an imaginary bug.

"How should I know?" Bugbite said mildly. "This isn't fairy work. We'd never make something that ugly."

It was still early in the day, and not many deputies had entered the Assembly Hall. But their numbers were increasing by the minute. Every time a deputy showed up to the session, she halted in the doorway, looked around with her mouth hanging open, and then rushed to join whichever of the milling, arguing groups with whom she had most affinity. But when Berkingmiddleshire appeared, she didn't stop, didn't gawk.

"Did you see that?" Syrene asked. "Not looking around at what everyone else is gawping at? It's the clearest tell. Berkingmiddleshire did it."

"She's very old. Maybe her eyesight is bad?" Una ventured.

"No," Lana said. "You're right, she did it."

The scribes weren't the only ones who noticed Berkingmiddleshire's suspicious behavior. An elderly politician hobbled up to the deputy, grabbed her by the collar, and began flinging curses. Two of Berkingmiddleshire's cronies leapt over the benches to support their friend, and from there, it was a brief downhill roll to a general brawl.

The louder the shouting, the more deputies joined the fray. Soon they were all pushing, jeering, jostling for position. Half of them were trying for a better view of the fight, the other half were screaming, demanding order. Fairies dropped down from the heights, brandishing their guns and weeping glitter.

At the edge of the scrum, Eloquentia was pleading with the daffodil fairy, communicating as much with her body as with words. On the far end of the room, the Speaker was doing the same, half kneeling in her throne, hands crossed over her heart, gazing up at the ruby-red fairy. Her wings jittered, soaking the Speaker in a waterfall of sparkles.

Bugbite stared down into the Assembly Hall, little face screwed up as if she was about to start crying. She gnawed on the tender tip of her nailless thumb. Lana put her arm around the fairy's hips.

"I was thinking of what you said the other day," Lana said in Bugbite's ear. "That fairies are scared of us."

"Who wouldn't be? You humans like this kind of thing. You're horrible."

With one flap of her wings, she shot up to the rafters. A backdraft of glitter exploded in Lana's face.

By the evidence, Lana couldn't disagree. The brawl was vastly entertaining. Napping was the scribes' favorite activity. It took something special for the scribes to give up the opportunity to catch up on their sleep while waiting for the day's session to begin. But all seven of them were squished into the front row, shoulder to shoulder, hanging over the railing.

It was as if they were on the second-floor gallery of the Ox-ford Arms, and the Butchers' Players were putting on a pan-tomime below. As the spectacle wore on, the librarians joined them, filling the row behind and standing on their tiptoes to get a better view.

"This has been a long time coming," Syrene announced. "That old Anglish girl is begging for a beating."

"Has been for two months," said Una.

The scribes and librarians all agreed. Then, one by one, each had a second thought. They stopped laughing and looked apologetically at Lana.

"It's nothing to me," Lana assured her fellow scribes. "Whenever we Anglish get our heads bashed in, it's generally no more than we deserve."

But Anglish heads weren't the only things getting bashed. Benches collapsed, desks smashed to kindling, chairs ripped from the floor and thrown. In the nearest corner, the deputies from Napule and Sicilia had Milano and Venesia by the hair. Under the Hanging Man, Bayern and Čechy clutched the throats of Savouè and Paris. All this because they couldn't get their hands on the Anglish deputies and were taking the next best option.

The Anglish had come with a plan. They weren't leaving themselves in the open. They had the wall at their back and a heavy bench obstructing access to their front. Lana sus-pected they wore some kind of armor under their robes. They had weapons, too—nothing as overt as a blade, but when anyone managed to get within striking distance, the Anglish laid them on the floor. Lead guessed, Lana suspected. Five deputies lay at their feet, and two more were crawling away.

Here and there, pages tried to clear routes to the doorways. Some deputies escaped to safety, but in general, chaos reigned.

It would have been natural enough for Lana to shrug off the implications of the brawl, take it for what it was worth, and enjoy the distraction. But this was bad. If the fairies noticed that real violence was being done, someone would get shot.

Lana waved her arms, trying to catch Eloquentia's eye. No luck. She was fully focused on the daffodil fairy.

No help to be found down there, but what about above? Up in the gallery rafters, Bugbite was miserable, shaking, shedding scales. Lana jumped on the bench.

"BB!" she shouted. "Come here."

When she opened her arms wide, the fairy didn't hesitate. She dove into Lana's arms.

"Grab your gun," Lana said.

She shifted Bugbite onto her hip with one arm and grabbed the gun with her other hand and pressed it into the fairy's fist.

"Shoot that one. Make her itch." She pointed at the deputy who had been throwing chairs. She now had the Speaker's gavel and looked keen to bash heads.

Bugbite lifted her gun, and the deputy dropped, scrabbling furiously under her robes.

"Now that one, and the idiots with her."

Lana pointed at Berkingmiddleshire. They fell, too, raking their robes with frenzied hands, scratching their necks and bellies.

It was like a marksmanship tournament. All she needed

to do was hold Bugbite steady and suggest targets. And even that was easy, because the scribes and librarians joined in as spotters, pointing and shouting.

Soon, all the worst aggressors were tormented by itches they could barely scratch. Deputies uninterested in fighting found safe and clear routes out of the Assembly Hall and exited at speed. Eloquentia hurried away without an upward glance.

When the Maréchal Assemblay arrived with five of her largest guards, there was nothing to do but locate the Speaker's missing gavel. The Maréchal took her elbow, and they both retreated into a passageway. The guards and pages began cleaning away debris.

The ruby fairy made a circuit of the hall. By the time she made it around to the scribes' gallery, Lana and her friends were all sitting at their desks with their hands folded, the picture of dutiful innocence.

"We're done here," Ruby said to Bugbite.

"Done for the day?" Lana asked. "Or done forever?"

The fairy spat. Three balls of hard red spittle bounced off Lana's boot in rapid succession. Lana jumped, shook her foot, winced.

"Hey, now," she said, louder than she'd meant.

"What happened to her face?" Ruby asked Bugbite. "She give you lip?"

"A misunderstanding with one of the kitchen staff," Lana said. Her foot throbbed. She was going to lose a toenail, for certain.

"Shut up, legger. Another word and I'll take out your eye."

Bugbite landed hard on Lana's shoulder and draped a wing over her face.

"No problem here, gracious Ruby," she said. "My scribes are diligent."

Her friend's wing was thin and soft as apricot skin. Lana scrabbled at it with gentle fingers, lifting the edge.

Ruby looked dubious.

"Diligent, are they? They're the only ones, then." She pointed at Bugbite rudely. "I put you on notice, scribe-wrangler. Don't get fond, because Parliament is going down."

12

Bugbite sat in the middle of the dinner table, legs crossed, chin in her hands. Her ragged petticoat had gotten so ripped and torn that it was now more of a decorative fringe than a garment.

"There's got to be a way out of here," said Lana. "Come on, think."

"We could steal a boat," said Margit.

"Does anyone know how to sail?" Lana asked. Everyone shook their heads.

"There are no boats anyway," said Melodia. "We could build a raft. That doesn't take much skill."

"A secret raft," said Una. "We could build it up on a rooftop."

"Where the fairies can see it," said Syrene. She rapped an imaginary hammer on the table. "Don't mind us, gracious beauties. We're just building a raft. Humans do that sometimes, you know. No particular reason."

"Too complicated anyway," said Vera. "We should just run for it. Head for high land."

"I told you before," said Bugbite. "The road's enchanted. It'll take you into mud pits and quicksand."

"Those weren't exactly your words," Syrene said. "You told

us we'd get dragged into a bottomless pit of quicksand, and the earth would shit our corpses out the other side."

"Nice, BB," Lana murmured.

"What if you came with us?" Una asked Bugbite. "You could guide us to safety."

The fairy didn't answer. She shook her head. A little cloud of glitter formed around her short black hair.

Raina Estrella kicked Lana under the table.

"Why wouldn't it work, BB?" Lana asked.

"It's an old enchantment, and that means it's strong," she said. "Human or fairy, if you leave without permission, you die. If I left, it'd make me fly higher and higher until my wings froze. Then I'd go splat. Don't you see, I'm stuck here, too?"

"But the difference is, you're not going to drown," said Syrene.

"That's a big difference," said Melodia.

"Yeah, but it's not my stupid government, is it?" A little of the old Bugbite flashed over the fairy's face: belligerent, nasty. Then she drooped.

Lana reached into her pocket. The scribes all brightened.

"Sorry," she said. "The yeast needs a few more days to re-bud enough for everyone. But I just remembered I didn't eat these." She pulled out the morning's mushroom scales and dropped them both on her tongue. "There's been enough arguing today. Come on, BB, let's go for a walk."

Lana knew the route to the courtyard now. In daylight, it seemed closer. Smaller, too.

"I made a good showing here, right?" Lana scuffed her boots through the scales Bugbite had dropped the night before, a constellation of garish stars, grounded and gone smash. "Though, now I'm thinking about it, Madam Deputy asked me to be subtle."

"She did."

"Ah, well. If you borrow a horse, you can't choose its gaits."

Lana skipped over a field of hallucinatory daisies and stuck her head through the doorway she'd seen Eloquentia use. The ground floor was a porter's storeroom, shelves of linen and candles shut away behind a counter. Lana leaned in and hallooed, which brought an old porter out from behind a stack of mops and brooms. Her head carried sad old donkey ears, furry and gray. A skylark jumped onto the porter's shoulder and began singing a fervent Tuscan aria.

"Hello, I'm looking for Madam Deputy de la Barre," Lana said, trying to keep her eyes from straying off to follow the next mushroom-induced vision.

"Third floor." The deputy raised her hand, and Lana had to take it on faith that she lifted three fingers, not the seven she saw.

Lana ran up the first flight of stairs, but Bugbite didn't follow. She had to turn right around and slide down the banister to find her friend where she'd left her, out in the courtyard. Her arms were crossed, shoulders high and stiff.

"Aren't you coming?"

Bugbite didn't answer. Storm clouds brewed on her forehead.

"Are you too shy? Is that it?"

The fairy huffed, breath fluttering her jagged bangs.

"You're shy around Eloquentia, aren't you? Madam Deputy, I mean. Here, this will help."

Lana shook out a few grains of yeast. She'd told the scribes the truth—it hadn't budded enough for all, but there was enough to take the edge off a fairy.

Bugbite licked her palm, and her shoulders released. A slow smile spread from the whiskers on one side to the whiskers on the other.

They ascended the staircase side by side. The third-floor foyer offered the choice of three doors. It took them five tries to find the right one, giggling and making a general ruckus.

When they finally identified Eloquentia's door, Bugbite zipped in close and put her eye up to the keyhole at the same time Lana shoved the door open. She stumbled over the fairy. They both landed in a heap on Madam Deputy's threshold sprawled at her slippered feet.

The large room had a gigantic pillar bed with peacock-patterned drapery. A tall brass candlestick stood beside it, wreathed in melted wax. Wilted flowers slumped in a creamy bowl on the windowsill, picked out with pinpoints of light from the latched shutters.

Eloquentia crossed the room to a little pedestal table and chair. The table was piled high with books and papers, littered with pens and pencils, scraps of sealing wax, and bits of ribbon. More books were piled in the room's corners, and the walls all had papers tacked to them or little booklets dangling from bits of string.

But that wasn't all. In front of Lana's nose were two buckets: one foamy with soap, the other leaking water into a puddle in the middle of the floor. Above, laundry hung on an improvised line strung between the doorjamb and the window shutter. Snowy bloomers, fine lawn shifts, and a dangle of stockings. The heels blushed pink and turned their shy faces to the wall.

"What a mess," Lana said, and immediately regretted it. "I mean, Madame Deputy, don't you have a maid?"

"I sent her home five days ago." Eloquentia retrieved a goblet from behind her stack of papers and sipped. "Most deputies have sent their attendants away. Parliament's failings aren't their fault. There's no reason they should suffer."

"Has Berkingmiddleshire?"

"I wouldn't know." Eloquentia looked frosty.

"Because that would show something, wouldn't it? If she sent her people home, it would show how far she was planning to take her grievance."

"I suppose that depends on her character." Eloquentia sipped again. "I couldn't say. I don't trust my judgment anymore."

She extended the tip of her finger and nudged the window shutter open. Daylight etched her laugh lines and crow's feet and emphasized the blue shadows under her eyes. Even exhausted and drawn tight like a bowstring ready to snap, Lana had never seen a beauty to match.

Eloquentia gave Bugbite and Lana a half-hearted smile.

"You are looking at an incompetent politician. I understand only a portion of any issue and never the most important piece. When there's a dispute, arguments take me by surprise. When there's a vote, I support the losing side."

"That can't be true," Bugbite breathed, too softly for Eloquentia to hear.

"Every side has been losing lately," Lana said. "Everything feels extra hopeless when you're tired."

"Tired, am I?" Eloquentia laughed. "But you don't know

the full story, either of you. I'm cracked and hollow in spirit. I've tried my best, and it hasn't been nearly enough. I've failed."

"Have you really tried, though?" Lana said.

Bugbite pinched her arm.

"Hey!" Lana exclaimed.

Sorry. Shut up, Bugbite mouthed, eyes wide and very serious.

Through her mushroom fugue, Lana slowly became aware that she and Bugbite were still on the floor, just inside the threshold. She scrambled to her feet. There was no place to sit, so Lana stood beside the laundry line, hands on her hips.

"You've hardly said a word in session. If you took the floor, nobody could stand against you. Nobody."

Eloquentia laughed again. Not a world-weary chuckle this time but a full guffaw. It went on for a long time. So long that Bugbite finally stopped looking frightened and joined Lana in the middle of the room, hovering at her shoulder.

"Though, now I'm thinking about it," Lana said when the dancer's laughter quieted. "I don't believe talking will solve this problem."

"Parliament is nothing but talking," Eloquentia said. "You don't see the half of it in the Assembly Hall. We talk all the time, in committees and working groups, all through the day and night. We negotiate, build alliances, wheedle. Especially, we lie."

"You lie?" Bugbite blurted, shocked.

"No, I don't." The dancer stared into the depths of her goblet. "I should learn. It might bring more success."

"They say all politicians are liars," said Lana.

"Not this one. Perhaps I'm not smart enough to lie."

"I doubt that." Lana tapped her chin with the tip of her forefinger. Behind a cloud, an idea was forming. "Berkingmiddleshire and her gang don't seem very smart, and yet they don't have any problem with lying, right, BB?"

The fairy didn't answer. Lana would have kept talking, but gazing at Bugbite's dear little face, she had to pause. How essential to her the fairy had become in such a short time. Maybe it was just the mushroom, but now Lana couldn't imagine her life without the fairy. Her ragged hair, garish wings, kinked and split whiskers, and broad, mobile face—all so precious. She'd begun calling the fairy *beauty* out of politeness, but she was beautiful—a precious individual and Lana's very best friend.

And right now, that friend was mulling something over, looking troubled.

"I don't want to say anything," the fairy said finally. "Because fairykin believes all humans are treacherous and never to be trusted." Bugbite clapped a hand over her mouth. "Oh shit."

"That's fair," Lana said. "Right, Eloquentia? I mean, Madam Deputy?"

"*Vraiment.* Don't trouble yourself, Beauty Bugbite."

The dancer pushed back her chair. She floated across the room to a wide trunk, unlocked it, and produced a wine bottle, half-empty, its cork protruding at an angle. She rummaged through the trunk to find two more goblets and then drifted back to retrieve her own.

"I don't have a fairy-size cup, my apologies. And I have only one chair, so I'll join you on the floor." She sat and shared out the bottle evenly, pouring the last dregs slowly so the sediment settled in the bottle's shoulder.

Bugbite managed the heavy goblet by leaving it on the floor and hovering horizontally, sipping as if from a pool. When the contents retreated beyond the reach of her lips and tongue, she tipped it and lapped at the edge.

Lana couldn't take her eyes off the process. Neither could Eloquentia. No more conversation, no more painful deep thoughts. Just two women sitting on the floor, watching a fairy negotiate a glass of wine.

"I hope you have another bottle," Lana said when her cup was empty.

Bugbite looked hopeful. Eloquentia smiled at them both and rose from the floor with admirable grace.

Lana reclined, propped up on an elbow, one leg bent. It was a good pose—casual, relaxed, offering any appreciative viewer an excellent perspective on her long legs.

The dancer pulled out another bottle.

"I've been saving this, though I can't remember why."

"Perhaps you were waiting for some worthy friends to drink with?" Lana said.

When they'd met in the courtyard, Eloquentia had baldly rejected Lana's attempts at gallantry. This time, she grinned. Maybe she even fluttered her lashes.

"Yes, that must be the case," she said, and filled all three goblets to the brim.

13

Lana never made it back to her own bed that night. She woke in a lady's boudoir, morning's soft light filtering through the shutters. The bed was large. There ought to have been plenty of space, but she was hanging over the edge. When she tried to turn over, she got an elbow in the nose. Bugbite's elbow.

"Good morning," Lana whispered.

The fairy didn't move. She was stretched out on her back, arms wide, legs splayed, wings akimbo. How could someone less than half the size of an adult woman take up so much room? But then, Lana had shared beds with her sisters all her life, and she knew a person's size was no indication of them being a comfortable bedmate.

On the other side of the bed, Eloquentia slept peacefully, face relaxed, hands tucked under her chin in a graceful pose. She wasn't squished. Bugbite had given her plenty of room.

"You little beast," Lana whispered. She had a cramp in her shoulder, a crick in her neck, and her foot was numb from dangling.

But to be fair, Lana had to admit if she'd been lucky enough to claim the middle, she would have crowded Bugbite over the side, too. Not because she didn't want to get close to the dancer but in hopes of being invited back.

Because nothing had happened between the three of them. Just the disposal of more bottles of wine along with several cheeses and a large loaf of bread. There had been a slow descent from sitting on the floor to lying on the floor, eventually followed by a convivial crawl toward bed.

Lana leaned close to Bugbite's ear and whispered at her to wake up. The fairy cracked an eye. She gazed at Lana blearily for a moment, then snapped awake and levitated from the bed. Lana crept to the door, her friend at her side. They both paused at the threshold and turned back.

"This seems wrong," Lana said. "Creeping out in the dark of night, leaving a sleeping lover unaware. I've never done it before."

"It's late morning. And she's not your lover. Not unless you have a long appendage I don't know about."

They argued. Eloquentia snored softly through it all. In the end, Bugbite slipped out the window, picked two roses from the fairies' breakfast hoard, and left them on the bed.

That satisfied Lana. Kept her smug and smiling all through her hangover and into the afternoon. She only became apprehensive up in the scribes' gallery, waiting for Eloquentia to appear, and worrying about how to greet her when she did.

It was the classic lover's dilemma. Lana wanted to be attentive without servility. She needed to show Eloquentia she was hopeful and bold, but not anxious or overbearing. And all this had to be communicated at a distance of three hundred feet or more.

She needn't have worried. The moment Eloquentia entered the Assembly Hall, she smiled up into the scribes' gallery. Lana imagined she would have waved, too, if she hadn't been carrying so many books and papers.

"She still likes us," said Lana.

"How could she not?" Bugbite replied.

Lana grinned. The fairy's nose was dusted with golden pollen. Lana swiped it gently away with the tip of her pinkie.

The deputy from Pivden Ukrayiny was pushing a proposal for a slight change to Black Sea fishing treaties. Now she had the floor, taking final questions before the Call for Decision. All seemed well. When the other deputies had questions, they spoke politely and in Fairy. Everyone seemed determined to be both serious and moderate. As the session ground on, the Speaker sat straighter and more confidently in her throne. Lana imagined she was breathing a sigh of relief, hoping a new day had dawned and the season of madness was finally over.

Then Berkingmiddleshire took the floor. Lana sighed and topped up her inkwell.

"Here is yet another example of unwarranted Fairy meddling. Fish swim where they please, and there is enough for all. But women are told where we may and may not go. Where are our inalienable rights and territories? What need have we for legislation that tells us where we may or may not fish?"

The deputy rasped at length, in Anglish. When she finally sat, her place was taken by Weigh-North-Yorking and then her other Anglish cronies, each one stirring confusion and dissent. All around, deputies murmured and passed comments up and down the rows. If they'd been cats, their fur would have been standing on end, backs arched, ears flat. Fairies speeded to and fro, brandishing guns and flooding the air with shed scales.

And Eloquentia, la députée de Dauphine-Provence? Eloquentia leaned over her desk and knocked her forehead on its surface three times.

When the vote came, Eloquentia paced to the Aye side. She was nearly alone there, accompanied only by deputies from Black Sea nations affected by the treaty. Many deputies abstained by staying seated; the rest stomped over to Nay. Another hung vote.

~

If Lana could be said to have made a plan to meet with Eloquentia that night, it was stifled by the Speaker and the Maréchal Assemblay, who ended the session well before midnight. At her request, the ruby fairy made an announcement. She hovered over the Speaker's chair with her gun on her shoulder and shouted in an impossibly high and ringing voice.

"A message from the Maréchal Assemblay. Those who care to walk down to the port may find some news about some of your missing colleagues."

The scribes trooped down together, taking a route from the library along sheer granite cliffs to the narrow mule path that led to the port. The moon had yet to rise, but the path was limed white and glowed in the light from the lantern Bugbite carried overhead.

The mule path joined a narrow road leading down to the port. Usually it would be deserted, but it was crowded with people, all hurrying in the same direction. Bevies of fairies darted overhead.

Bugbite returned to Lana's shoulder.

"This is not going to be pretty," she said.

Lana had been thinking the same thing.

"Bodies?" she asked, and the fairy nodded. "We should stick together," she said to the other scribes, but they had already linked arms, making a tight chain.

Lana attached herself to one end and hugged Syrene's arm to her ribs. She took the lantern from Bugbite, too. It was no burden to her, but for Bugbite, it must have been a load.

There was no getting down to the port—it was already too crowded. But they could see everything from the stretch of road above the last hairpin turn. A potbellied Breton fishing boat snugged up to the jetty. Lanterns hung from its yards and masts, illuminating pairs of sailors who hauled large, canvas-shrouded bundles from the deck and laid them in rows on the wharf. Fairies were everywhere overhead. Some held lanterns, some conjured balls of light and focused the beams on the wharf. Most just watched.

When the sailors laid the last body down, there were eight in total. The Maréchal Assemblay knelt beside each of the corpses in turn and peeled back each shroud to reveal the faces. Some were fish-bitten, their features now simple holes in gray faces. Some were masked in mud, their mouths gaping in endless screams. The last two were girls, still children, really, barely full grown. They lay fresh on the planks like enchanted princesses from some old tale.

A voice rose from the crowd.

"This is what happens when fairies govern. In a few days, we'll all be thus."

"No," said the Speaker, who had joined the Maréchal

Assemblay corpse-side. "This is what happens when people run away without permission to leave."

"Give us permission, then," said another woman, her voice high and tense. "Keep your deputies, but let the rest of us go. We don't need to drown because of your incompetence."

Another voice rose over hers, threatening.

"Whether you let us go or not, you can cook your own damn meals or starve."

A hum from the crowd, many voices speaking at once, multiplying to a roar. As one, the fairies rose, fleeing the sound. One dropped her lantern, and another dove to catch it before it hit the crowd. Within moments, all fairies were high overhead, their lights barely brighter than stars.

Bugbite stayed. She clapped her hands over her ears and winced. Scales fell from her wings.

"Go!" Lana yelled. She didn't dare grab the fairy, so she had to make do with flinging her arm skyward, pointing. "Get out of this. Go!"

The fairy launched herself high, scales trailing behind like a comet.

Lana wrapped her arms around Raina Estrella and Syrene, who clung to the other four. A little knot of scribe-kind in the howling mass—howling? No. Keening, for the sound was as much grief as anger. It echoed off the cliffs above. When it reached the tidal shores of Bretagne and Angleterre, the villagers would never recognize the sound as human. They'd hide behind their doors and shutters, singing prayers and wards against demons and dread things of the night.

But here was nothing supernatural. Just human rules and human folly, enforced by fairies.

The Speaker and the Maréchal Assemblay covered the corpses' faces. They stood with lowered heads, letting the crowd's emotions wash over them, waiting for it to ebb like the tide. No need for guards; they could never stand against such a crowd anyway.

Every mother's daughter knows anger and grief must have their say.

Lana hadn't forgotten to look for Eloquentia. She stood behind, higher in the road. She carried a lantern, but the hood of her cloak eclipsed her expression. She was safe, though, the crowd around her thin, and Lana knew she was nimble enough to get away if the crowd turned violent.

It didn't, though, perhaps out of respect for the dead. When the Speaker and the Maréchal Assemblay finished paying their respects, the Maréchal spread her heavy arms wide, gesturing for quiet. It took several repetitions, but eventually she was able to shout and be heard. Her voice was authoritative.

"Everyone not directly involved with the order of Parliament has permission to leave."

A roar of surprise, then joy. The Maréchal waited for the noise to subside before gesturing for quiet again.

"To be clear, deputies and pages must stay, along with librarians—"

Lana's inner voice screamed the next words before the Maréchal even said them.

"—and scribes."

14

Lana and Bugbite rose early and raided the abandoned kitchens. They giggled all the way, giddy from lack of sleep and goaded by a few grains of newly budded yeast. By evening, Lana judged, she'd have enough to offer the other scribes a little mood lifter.

In the meantime, the scribes woke to a table piled high with wheels of cheese, bread loaves, terra-cotta jugs of olives, and at least twenty yards of sausage links—enough to tie up the Maréchal Assemblay and three of her guards.

"Let's revisit the raft idea. Maybe we can find some pig bladders," said Lana at breakfast.

This was met by downturned mouths and baleful stares.

They say drowning is a kind death. That's what Lana had told her mother in her first—and only—letter home. But even under-slept and silly, she had the sense not to repeat it at breakfast.

"Where's the beer?" asked Syrene. "I'm not facing any of this sober."

"Parliament beer will never get you drunk and you know it," said Raina Estrella. Her eyes weren't open yet. She felt her way across the room and laid her upper body across the table.

"It can if I drink enough of it," said Syrene darkly.

"No beer," said Bugbite. "It's locked in the cellars. I don't have a key. Don't know who does."

"The Maréchal Assemblay," Una growled.

"Who's fetching and carrying for the deputies?" asked Vera. "They're not getting their own breakfasts, no chance."

"The pages, of course," said Raina Estrella.

"Does that mean the librarians should climb up and down stairs for us?" asked Una.

"Hush, hush," said Bugbite.

For a moment, the fairy sounded like a fond mother quieting her children. Then she took a mushroom from her pocket and passed it around. Only Una refused—it gave her scary dreams, she said, but the others set upon it like ants on honey.

This meant all the scribes except Una were happily distracted as they trooped into Parliament and took their usual places in the gallery. If they stared with fascination at dark corners, or gazed into the rafters and giggled, so be it. It was better than suffering with dread about a mess they couldn't fix. Or so Lana said to Bugbite.

"Is it better, though?" the fairy asked. "I'm afraid it might be unkind kindness. Do humans have those? It's when you do something that helps another person misbehave."

"BB," Lana said with great affection, "you just defined our entire relationship."

The Maréchal Assemblay and her guards marshaled the pages like soldiers, lining them up in front of the Speaker's throne and lecturing them. Laying down the law, obviously.

The Speaker hadn't slept, that was clear from the huge blue circles under her eyes that extended halfway to her mouth.

She hadn't the benefit of mushrooms to calm her nerves and take her mind off her troubles. No, even at a distance, Lana could tell her hands were shaking.

And the ruby fairy and all her friends? They hovered in clumps overhead, brandishing their guns with verve, eager for an excuse to start firing.

No stragglers, no latecomers today. All the deputies marched in on time, po-faced or scowling. One or two looked ready to burst into tears. Not Eloquentia. She was serious, collected. Lana was ready to meet her gaze with similar heroism, but she didn't look up.

As the Speaker prepared to call for order, the other six scribes joined Lana and Bugbite at the front of the gallery. Lana was pleased to have Raina Estrella's comfortable presence back at her side. Syrene and Vera joined them in the front row, and the other three huddled close behind. They opened their journals, filled their inkwells, and sat with pens ready.

The Maréchal Assemblay handed the gavel to the Speaker. One concussion would have been enough to quiet the Assembly Hall, but she repeated the gesture again, and again, a dozen times, slow and regular as the tolling of a bell. When the sound finally stopped, the very foundations of Parliament seemed to hold its breath.

"There will be no shenanigans," said the Speaker. "All will respect the solemnity of Parliament and the two hundred and fifty years of peace it has brought. To that end, here are your instructions. All pending votes will receive a two-thirds majority for Yea or for Nay. There will be no hung votes."

She emphasized the last three words with three slams of

her gavel. After pausing to let the noise resound, she then banged it once more for good measure.

"To that end, the deputies have voluntarily formed three temporary parties of exactly equal size and have sworn to vote Yea or Nay according to the instruction of their party whips. This is a temporary emergency measure. If successful, with further usage, it may create a precedent for future Parliamentary operations. That is not our intent, however. This measure is adopted to ensure that this honorable House"— her voice broke—"remains as solid, permanent, and formidable as the rock it is built on."

The Speaker might be a talented politician with a lifetime of oratorial experience behind her, but the past weeks had taken its toll. If the corpses on the wharf had loosened her hinges, Lana understood completely.

"I repeat," the Speaker said in a high and fractured voice, "there will be no damned tomfoolery. If any deputy breaks party lines, I'll personally string them up there."

She swung her gavel at the Hanging Man. A green fairy was perched on one of his arms, gun on her shoulder, and looked alarmed to be suddenly the center of attention.

With that final gesture, all energy drained out of the Speaker. She fell into her seat. Her voice turned thin and strained, like the wind whistling through a broken shutter.

"If Parliament can't cooperate to save itself," she said, "perhaps we deserve to drown."

Lana leaned close to Bugbite.

"Can they tell deputies how to vote?" she whispered.

"I dunno," the fairy said. "Your rules make little sense to me at the best of times."

~

Cooperate the deputies did, at least as long as daylight held. The three factions held steady for hours, voting on four separate Calls for Decision with, as far as Lana could tell, a reasonable imitation of sense. When she wasn't watching Eloquentia, Lana kept an eye on Berkingmiddleshire, Weigh-North-Yorking, and the rest of her troublesome fellow Anglish. They kept quiet, voted with their parties, and seemed to cause no trouble. Lana suspected they were just biding their time.

Night approached. As the light through the high windows began to fail, the scribes lit their candles. The dusty air of the gallery filled with the sweet scent of beeswax. Lana expected the lamplighters to troop into the Assembly Hall as usual, but nobody came. The Assembly Hall grew dimmer.

In the dark, the deputies' tempers began to fray. Some fairies conjured lights, but this didn't please the deputies. They shaded their eyes against the glare and barked complaints.

Arguments broke out, isolated and in hushed voices at first, but threatening to grow louder and spread. Pages ran in search of lamplighter's sticks and wicks. Before they could return, though, the Speaker called a recess. After a brief consultation with the Maréchal Assemblay, she closed the session.

"Few of the deputies have slept. I will not risk the integrity of this House on the temperament of exhausted politicians. You have done well. Come back tomorrow, refreshed and ready to work a full session."

She struggled to her feet and swayed. The Maréchal darted

to her side, propped her up, and helped her down from her throne.

When the scribes closed their journals, the librarians were already waiting to collect them. How long had they been standing at the back of the scribes' gallery? Lana couldn't tell, but she invited them to supper.

"There's only five of you. Aren't you lonely? Come have some good cheer."

It took a little pressing, but with encouragement from scribal bookworms Margit and Vera, the librarians relented. The extra bodies at supper meant the after-dinner yeast would be spread too thin to distribute, but one of the librarians had brought a large bottle of raki. Under its thick, age-stained glass, the liquor swirled with lemon rind and rosemary needles. Lana's first sip went straight to the back of her skull.

"Does everyone at Parliament have a secret stash?" Lana asked. She turned to Raina Estrella. "Where's yours?"

"My vices aren't for sharing," she said, then giggled. "Usually."

As the raki was poured, Lana let her cup be topped up to the brim. She sipped enough off so she could carry it without spilling, then clapped her palm over the cup's lip to be sure.

"You know what I'm thinking," she told Bugbite.

The fairy grabbed a sausage. Lana claimed a hunk of cheese. They wrapped the food in a clean handkerchief and set off toward Eloquentia's room.

Quiet near the kitchens, deserted in the halls and passages. Most windows were dark and shuttered. The moon overhead had waned to a sliver, its orb divided and subdivided to a slender fingernail paring. Tomorrow, a new moon would rise. It would be a dark night. A night for bat flight. For owls on the hunt. Witches would fly and politicians would make their last stand, for good or bad, for comedy or tragedy.

No porter at the bottom of Eloquentia's stairs. No noise but the creak of steps under Lana's feet. Eloquentia answered their knock dressed for bed in lawn shift and slippers, her hair combed into a cloud of dispersed curls. It frothed down her back in a cascade, the silver hairs among the dark. Lana knew this was no moment for flirting, but she put her free hand over her heart anyway—how could she not?—and offered the cup of raki.

"We thought you might not be provisioned," she said.

"And we brought food, too," Bugbite said. She pushed the bundle of sausage and cheese onto Eloquentia's chest.

"Thank you," the deputy said. "This will put me right to sleep."

It was as clear a dismissal as Lana had ever heard. She was half-ready to wish Eloquentia good night and turn away, but the dancer stepped back from the door and swept her arm, inviting them inside.

"No deputy deserves such kindness," she said. "Not today. Not tomorrow. Perhaps not ever."

"Today went well," Lana said. "Scribes follow every word, you know. It was a success. The best day at Parliament I've ever witnessed."

"Yes, I saw you." Eloquentia laughed at Lana's reaction. "Don't look so shocked. Each time I raised my eyes to the scribes' gallery, you were hard at work. And you, too, Beauty Bugbite, fetching and carrying for your team, bolstering their spirits. The scribes are lucky to have a friend like you."

"It's a new habit." Bugbite looked a little shamefaced.

"Better learned now than never."

The deputy pulled her chair to the bedside. She gestured for Lana to take the chair, then sat at the edge of the bed and patted the peacock quilt, encouraging Bugbite to sit, too. She sipped the raki and passed the cup to Lana, then picked at the sausage. A few morsels, only.

"It'll give me bad dreams," she said. "But the liquor will make me sleep like a child. Thank you."

Lana took only the tiniest sip to be polite and passed the cup to the fairy. Bugbite, too, sipped sparingly. When the dancer tried to pass the cup again, they both refused.

"I have a Call for Decision on the docket tomorrow, do you know that?" Lana and Bugbite shook their heads. "It's not important. Or, rather, I don't care about it anymore. When I introduced it to the schedule months ago, I trusted Parliament. I really did."

She rose from the bed and paced. Orating now, her whole body involved in her words.

"I was naïve. I thought that what deputies said was what they meant, allowing for the usual helping of human folly and blunder."

Eloquentia drank deep from the cup.

"I feel like a child," Eloquentia said with fervor. "The machinations of Parliament are beyond my understanding, and every move I make is foolish."

"Hey, now," Lana said, trying for a soothing tone. "Today was a good day. Remember?"

"Oh yes. Six hours of order, and then the Speaker curtailed

the session." Sarcasm thickened the air. With a sweep of her arm, Eloquentia drained the cup and pitched it into the cold hearth. "She knew if we had kept going, Parliament would disintegrate into dissent, confusion, and conflict interminable. And then death for us all."

The dancer collapsed back on the bed and put her face in her hands.

"The deputies needed to sleep," Bugbite said, very gentle. "So do you."

"Do you think that's what the Anglish are doing?" Eloquentia spoke through her fingers. "No, they're concocting their final plot, whatever that might be. And my stupid little Call for Decision will be square in the middle of it."

"They want dissolution," Lana said. "That's why it's so difficult to figure out. Confusion and hung votes are exactly what they want."

Lana blinked, surprised at her own insight. When she came back to herself, both Eloquentia and Bugbite were squinting at her.

Lana leaned the chair back against the wall, balancing it on two legs like she did at home, with Mother's favorite chair. She was terribly proud of herself, feeling like the master of the world. This must be what playing chess was like, if she'd ever bothered to learn. All the pieces at her command, their movements foreseeable many turns into the future.

"Berkingmiddleshire won't start the day by ruining every vote. Chaos is more effective in contrast with calm. And what they want is to push fairies over the edge. They want to die."

Bugbite folded her wings around herself and rolled on the bed, moaning.

"No, no, no. That's stupid."

"Humans are stupid, BB. You've said it yourself." Lana could hardly keep from rocking the chair back and forth with glee. "What they want, ultimately, is for all of Europe to rise against the fairies. The destruction of Parliament is their ultimate goal."

The dancer and the fairy gaped at Lana, mouths slack. Lana snapped her fingers in their faces.

"When is your vote coming up, Eloquentia? Madam Deputy, I mean."

"My stupid, useless Call for Decision? The Speaker will decide the order."

"Can you request a spot? Get it moved to fifth place?"

"In theory." Eloquentia's voice rose. "But why on earth would I want to do that? And why would the Speaker allow it? She and the Maréchal Assemblay will be chewing over the schedule all night, trying to save us all."

Lana let her chair topple back onto four legs. She reached out and took the dancer's flailing hands. It was the first time they'd touched. Though Lana had imagined it many times, she'd never predicted this scenario: Eloquentia upset, Lana the calm, wise counselor, and Bugbite playing the part of doubtful co-conspirator.

The dancer's hands were cold. Lana gathered them to her chest and covered them with her own.

"The Speaker can't do anything; neither can the Maréchal. If they could, they would have already," Lana told her. "It's up to you. You're going to save Parliament."

15

Discord had been sown in the night. The deputies who, only yesterday, had entered the Assembly Hall full of calm purpose were now fractured in spirit, tempers torn. None of them chatted as they entered the Assembly Hall, and few walked in pairs. They stayed as far away from one another as they could. Many actually changed their seats to put room between themselves and their neighbors.

"Maybe the Speaker shouldn't have sent them to bed, after all," said Syrene.

The scribes and librarians packed themselves into the front row of desks, sitting on shoulder-to-shoulder and leaning over the railings to watch the procession of deputies.

"I think they're just hungover," Lana said. "Everyone has a secret stash, right?"

"It's a miserable job," said Una. "If I had to be a deputy, I'd be drunk all the time."

"I bet some of them are," said Melodia.

"That's why they're all useless," said Vera. "The only people willing to take on the job are grasping for power."

"What power, though?" said Una. "It's not like they can do anything real. Any neighborhood brewster has more power than a deputy."

"The power to make history?" suggested one of the librarians.

"Or to end it," said Syrene grimly.

When Eloquentia crossed the threshold, she looked collected, if a little tense, but she'd forgotten to fasten the front of her robe. Peony-pink satin flashed behind the purple wool.

"They're not all stupid," said Lana. "Some of them are wonderful."

"And some aren't."

Berkingmiddleshire entered looking smug and self-satisfied. Usually, her bony form poked acute angles in the shoulders of her robes, but today, she was padded as if dressed for winter.

"Is she wearing floats?" Lana asked.

All the scribes and librarians watched the deputy cross the floor. When she took her seat, her arms rested at an unnatural angle as if propped.

"Looks like it," said Raina Estrella. "How is that fair, Beauty Bugbite? She gets to float and we don't?"

"Don't look at me. I didn't give them to her." The fairy put her arm around Lana's shoulders and whispered in her ear, "Looks like she's planning to make short work of the votes."

All the Anglish deputies were similarly padded under their robes. It was especially noticeable on Heregloucester, who looked as though she were pregnant with twins and carrying them in her armpits.

Raina Estrella waved to catch the eye of her page. She puffed out her cheeks and canted her elbows, rocking back and forth as if on a wave. The page frowned and looked away, confused.

"They don't notice it down below," Lana said. "We can see things up here that they can't."

For example, Lana could watch every move Eloquentia made. She saw her signal to a page, send her with a note to the Speaker.

"That's the docket order request," Bugbite whispered to Lana.

The plan they'd made last night with Eloquentia was simple, but it hinged on a guess—that Berkingmiddleshire wouldn't begin the day forcing hung votes. Lana figured she'd bide her time, let a few votes pass before making her move. Short of pulling out a sword and gutting the deputies one by one, surprise and confusion were really the only weapons in the Anglish arsenal. If they began the day with a frontal attack, they'd give away the game, and the Speaker would have a long time to regroup.

The question was, how many good votes would the Anglish let through before making their move? No more than two or three, Eloquentia had suggested. Perhaps four, if they felt very confident.

The Maréchal Assemblay and the Speaker entered the room together, escorted by four guards. The Speaker looked frail and thin, and leaned all her weight on the Maréchal's arm. When she settled into her throne, the ruby fairy fluttered down from the rafters. She had two guns now, one in each hand, and waved them like clubs.

"The Maréchal could backhand little Ruby across the room," said Syrene. "Just like that."

Bugbite winced. She still had her arm around Lana's neck. Lana felt a shudder course through the fairy's whole body.

"Hey, now," Lana said.

"I'm sorry, Beauty, but the Speaker is older than my onna," Syrene added. "Ruby should have some respect."

"Fairykin are old, too," said Bugbite.

Lana patted the fairy's hand.

"Remember, nobody's having fun here. Right?" Lana said. Everyone nodded. "It's going to be a long day. Let's stay neighborly."

It was the maturest thing Lana had ever heard come out of her own mouth. If she ever made it home to London, nobody would believe it.

The Speaker's strategy seemed to be to pretend it was just another Parliamentary day, as if sticking close to custom would make everything run smoothly. She opened the session, made some administrative announcements, including a precis of the temporary voting parties established the previous day, and then announced the first Call for Decision on the docket.

So far so good, Lana figured, except that when the Speaker invited the deputy sponsoring the call to take the floor, nobody stood.

"Baja-Sombor," the pages called as they ran up and down the aisles.

One of the youngest pages actually looked up at the Hanging Man, as if the missing deputy might be keeping company with that ancient icon. If Lana could have found any humor in the moment, she would have laughed. As it was, it chilled her. Even the sight of Eloquentia looking up into the scribes' gallery didn't warm her.

We guessed wrong, Eloquentia mouthed.

"It's not over yet," Bugbite whispered.

As the Maréchal and her guards stomped out to search for the deputy from Baja-Sombor, fairies flitted up and down the aisles, counting the deputies. When each of them came up with a different number, the Speaker rose from her throne.

"Whips will form their party members into groups for the purpose of enumeration."

Groans from the deputies. General chaos as they gathered their papers and moved to new seats. The change was good from Lana's perspective, because Eloquentia's full profile was now visible instead of the back of her head, and she was a little closer, too. But her expression was bleak.

Lana didn't bother counting heads. The other scribes were doing it. And the numbers were not encouraging. Three deputies were missing, and not one from each party, either, but two from one party and one from another. Exactly the best way to make the Speaker's solution inoperable.

When the Maréchal returned, grim-faced and empty-handed, the Speaker had no choice.

"The parties are dissolved. Deputies may vote at will."

Berkingmiddleshire stood and cast her arms wide.

"You twist the customs and precedents of Parliament to suit fairy demands. This ancient tree might once have borne good fruit, but fairies have tortured it into rot and disease."

"Sit down. You are not recognized." The Speaker's voice was weak and barely carried. The deputy spoke over her.

"This House has no ability to govern. I move a vote of no confidence."

Half the deputies surged to their feet, yelling and waving their hats. The others shrank into their seats. No prize for guessing which group Eloquentia was in. Her face was gray with horror, her hands knotted in her lap.

"Parliament should be dissolved!" screamed Berkingmiddleshire. "No more fairy tyranny!"

Her cronies took up the chant, banging their desks. "No more fairy tyranny! No more fairy tyranny!"

Like birds flocking, the fairies who had been flitting chaotically above the deputies coalesced into a spiral. They raised their guns. Light flashed along the barrels and beyond, sparks speeding with one target: Berkingmiddleshire. The deputy fell.

She toppled forward, falling face-first from the first row onto the floor. Sudden, shocked silence, then one lone scream from the back of the House.

The Maréchal grabbed the Speaker's gavel and began laying into the side of the mace's velvet-covered stand with all her body as if intending to build a boat at speed.

"Quiet and order," she demanded. "Guards, remove Berkingmiddleshire from the Assembly."

But Berkingmiddleshire would be alive for only a moment more. Even from a distance, the scribes could see that. Blood, so much of it, soaked her robes through. From her crumpled position, the deputy lifted her knee. Her arm drew a wing of blood on the floor. And then she moved no more.

When the guards dragged the body away, it left a trail of gore across the Assembly Hall's checkered floor.

The scribes huddled together, shocked and silent. When Lana reached for Bugbite, she found only air. Her fairy friend had hung on her neck all morning, but now she was gone. Lana twisted, searching for her in the rafters. Had Bugbite joined the fairy executioners?

"BB, no," Lana said under her breath.

"Who will stand for Berkingmiddleshire?" said the Speaker, her voice thin and strained. Silence reigned then. "Is there a page who calls it home? Must someone claim the proxy?"

So many pages, it was hard for Lana to believe they wouldn't find a fellow Anglish in the crowd. The Speaker and the Maréchal put their heads together. A page with a wet rag swiped at the blood on the floor.

"That one has never cleaned kitchen flags," said Syrene in a flat voice.

The other scribes nodded. The page was efficient at moving the blood around, but not mopping it up. Soon, she would find herself at the center of a thin-spread circle of blood, dried and flaking. The smeared edges were turning brown already.

Eloquentia stood.

"With permission, Madam Speaker," she said. "A proxy is not necessary. This House has a mechanical from Berkingmiddleshire."

A sob from above. There was Bugbite, hiding on a rafter, clutching her gun like a doll.

"What are you doing up there?" Lana scolded. "Come down."

The fairy shook her head, and a slow cascade of green and yellow flecks filtered down on the scribes. Lana brushed it from her lapels and sighed.

"Fairies are so stubborn," she said. And then she realized all the scribes were looking at her. "What?" she asked.

"A mechanical from Berkingmiddleshire," said Raina Estrella. "That's you."

"Me?" Lana poked her thumb into her chest. "I'm from London."

"London is part of Berkingmiddleshire," said Una.

"That rude corpse was one of your own, you twit," said Syrene.

Down on the floor, Eloquentia was staring up at her, eyes over-wide. *Say something,* she mouthed.

"I'm a London girl!" Lana yelled. "Will that do, madams?"

"No, no, no," Bugbite sobbed from above.

Raina Estrella elbowed Lana in the ribs.

"You're not supposed to talk unless you're on your feet."

Lana stood. She was about to repeat herself, but the Speaker wasn't insisting on ceremony, and the Maréchal was already sending pages to fetch her. Tall ones, and they didn't look friendly at all.

~

"Hey, now. I'm doing you a favor, remember?"

The pages wrestled Lana into a purple deputy's robe and slammed one of the big mushroom caps over her head. The page who insisted on fumbling with Lana's buttons was not giving up the job, no matter how many times Lana tried to nudge her fingers aside and do the buttons herself.

The deeply creased robe reeked of must and rosemary. It had probably been sitting in the bottom of a chest for years. The hat was no better. Lana swiped it off her head.

"The chapeau is optional, right? Not all the deputies wear it."

"Juniors do." A short page with pointy shoulders yanked the cap back over Lana's ears. "It's so the Speaker can pick the idiots out of the crowd."

"Doesn't work, though," said another page. "All the deputies are stupid."

"Surely not all," said Lana, thinking of Eloquentia.

"Oh yes. Each deputy a dunce," the pages chorused. It was clearly one of their favorite mottos.

"And I'm the dimmest of them all now." Lana nodded. "Good to know. That helps."

She let the pages push her through the grand doorway and onto the Assembly Hall floor. The space looked so much bigger from below, the banks of benches steeper, the vaulted ceiling higher, and the air positively crowded with fairies. At first, she thought they didn't have guns, but that was only because the weapons were all pointed at Lana's own head.

The pages tried to hustle her into the nearest empty seat, but Lana dodged them and charged across the floor toward Eloquentia. She half expected the pages to give chase, but they let her go. She slowed to a dignified walk instead of tearing across the room as if trying to catch a chicken.

All eyes were on Lana, but the only gaze she cared about was Eloquentia's. That perfect face, her gentle, patient smile, her so-soft skin—just one glance was as potent a drug as Lana ever dreamed of. Mesmerized, she slid slowly onto the green bench and took her place at the dancer's side.

Eloquentia leaned in. Her cherry-stained lips parted, ready to speak secrets for Lana's ears alone.

"The Speaker has to swear you in," she whispered.

If any of the deputies and pages hadn't seen her run across

the Assembly Hall all the first time, they certainly saw her retrace her steps to be sworn in. Lana's ears burned as she promised to be a faithful deputy for Berkingmiddleshire and all her chattels. They were still burning as she crossed the floor the third time, and took her seat again.

"I'm sorry," Eloquentia whispered. "But the Speaker would have had to give Berkingmiddleshire's proxy to one of her Anglish cronies."

"It's fine," Lana said. The tips of her ears glowed like coals, mere inches from Eloquentia's face. She tugged her cap lower. "I figure I can't do any worse than my predecessor. All I have to do is vote against horror and dissolution, right?"

The Speaker called for replacements for the other three missing deputies. Two pages volunteered, along with an ancient archivist who'd crept out from so deep in the stacks her very joints seemed to exude dust and silverfish. Lana swept off her mushroom cap and tossed it to the floor.

"I'm not junior anymore," she told Eloquentia.

"In the absence of the originator, this Official House decrees that Baja-Sombor's Call for Decision will be read as it stands."

The Speaker deputized the Maréchal Assemblay. When she took the floor, her imposing form was magisterial, but her voice, though loud, was monotonous. The content of the call didn't help. Something about building a new bridge over the river Duna—an issue essential no doubt to . . . to whom? To the people who lived in the vicinity, certainly, wherever that was. Spain? Finland?

"Pay attention," Eloquentia said, leaning close. Her breath tickled Lana's ear. "This is important."

"Is it, though?" Lana was willing to take its importance on faith, but if Eloquentia was feeling chatty, Lana could only encourage her.

"The river Duna has many names. We call it the Danube, as you know."

"Yes, of course," Lana lied. She'd heard of the Danube. It was somewhere east, she thought.

"The bridge will be important to Srbi, Madari, Hrvati, and the many other linguistic groups in the area. Which means . . ." Eloquentia opened her hand and spread her graceful fingers as if holding a golden apple.

"It means they all hate each other," Lana said.

Eloquentia coughed.

"I wouldn't say that. But it means that if we put the bridge in the wrong location, the consequences could be dire. So listen. Every word of that Call for Decision has been renegotiated a dozen times."

Lana crossed her ankles and leaned back in her seat. It was comfortable enough. Padded, unlike the scribes' benches. No need to sit on her hat, but she picked the great mushroomy thing off the floor anyway and placed it behind her lower back for a bit more support. And she tried to listen. Really, she did.

Was it her fault that the Maréchal's voice was sleep-inducing? She could hire herself out to insomniacs, because even on this day of days, in the bear pit of Parliament, with murderous fairies swirling overhead, and mere inches from the most desirable woman in the world, Lana was bored halfway to snoring.

"Are you okay?"

Bugbite's voice in her ear. Lana turned, and there was her friend perched behind her left shoulder, gnawing on the nail-less tip of her thumb as if working toward biting it off.

"You made it down from your rafter," Lana observed approvingly. "Well done, BB. I thought you were stuck there overnight."

"Do you need anything?"

"I need the Maréchal to shut up. Does that count?" Bugbite shook her head. "I'm good. Maybe Madame Deputy needs something, though?"

Eloquentia's gaze was locked on the Speaker.

"Hush," she said. "The vote is being called."

"Oh, the vote." Lana rolled her eyes. She wouldn't dare if Eloquentia was looking, but Bugbite giggled, and that pleased her.

When the Speaker called the vote, Lana followed Eloquentia to the Aye side. Once there, the deputy gripped Lana's elbow and pressed her nose into Lana's ear in a way she might have found sensual if her kinks involved sisterly scoldings.

"If you can't take this seriously," the deputy hissed, "just give me your proxy and recuse yourself."

"I've voted," Lana said mildly. "And unless you're a lot more conflicted than you seem, you must approve of the side I've taken."

"Yes, but if only you could be serious," Eloquentia repeated.

Deputies crowded around them, jostling for space with the Ayes while chattering in every language. Eloquentia's eyes glittered—clearly she was terribly upset. Lana itched to embrace her. A long, comforting hug with no funny business, that's what was required. Eloquentia's head would fit right under Lana's chin. All she needed to do was reach out and pull the dancer to her side. But no. Here, in the middle of This Officious House, with deputies all around, it was neither the time nor the place.

The Maréchal shouted for quiet. She'd taken the Speaker's gavel, apparently, and somewhere beyond the mass of Ayes was using it to build a cowshed.

"The vote is found hung," said the Speaker, and the room fell silent.

Some of the deputies began weeping. On Lana's right elbow was an ancient girl with white hair and a face like a dried mushroom. When she sank toward the floor, Lana snaked her arm around her waist and gathered her bony weight onto her breast. She would have reached for Eloquentia, too, but the milling of the deputies had pushed her out of reach.

Lana patted the ancient girl's hair. Death was creeping that much closer to Parliament, and Lana could smell its cold and fetid breath.

16

As soon as Lana and Eloquentia got back to their seats, Lana took her pens out. She tapped her precious blue enamel pen on the edge of the seat in front of her—one, two, three—before carefully unscrewing its golden finial. The penmaker had designed it specially for Lana. A little tiny globe with the continents sketched out in fine engraving.

"When I was young, I wanted to travel," she told Eloquentia, who was still looking both teary and angry, in that gorgeous way some women seemed to manage. "See the other side of the world and beyond. Meet girls from far away and kiss them." Lana smiled wistfully. "Or admire them from afar, at least."

Eloquentia was busy staring at the Speaker and the Maréchal, but she allowed herself to be cajoled. A shade of seriousness dropped from her expression, and a hint of a dimple appeared on her cheek, but she didn't look away from the Speaker's throne.

"I think looking at a pretty girl is even better than kissing her," said Bugbite. "The heart enjoys an expanse of possibilities."

Lana leaned back toward the fairy. She tipped a little yeast out onto her palm.

"That's a good philosophy, BB," Lana said, offering the yeast to her fairy friend. "The world is full of marvels. We'd be fools not to appreciate them."

Bugbite picked a few grains and dropped them onto her tongue. Lana held her hand out to Eloquentia, smooth and gallant, as if she were a tavern keeper offering her finest tipple to a favored guest.

Eloquentia glanced at Lana's hand. She looked away, uninterested, and then her gaze snapped back, narrow and piercing.

"Go ahead," said Bugbite, smiling in euphoria. "Honestly, Madam Deputy. It makes this ongoing disaster a lot easier."

"At least if you drown, you'll drown happy," Lana said, and inched her hand that much closer. "Where's the damage?"

Eloquentia crossed her arms and looked them both up and down.

"You told me last night I was going to save Parliament."

"Did we?" Lana asked Bugbite.

"Lana did," said the fairy. "I didn't."

"No plan survives contact with the enemy," Lana said. She nudged Eloquentia's elbow with the fingers of her outstretched hand. Short of an embrace, it was the best comfort she could offer. "You can plan and strategize and second-guess yourself all the way to the grave. But in the end, everyone follows their heart." Lana impressed herself. Here she was, a deputy in Parliament, straight and upright as her mother could wish, and passing along wisdom to her betters. "What does your heart want?" she asked.

"My heart?" Eloquentia repeated.

"What does it tell you?" Bugbite asked, gently.

The deputy chuckled. She raised her hand to her brow as if exhausted.

"My heart tells me that as stupid and frustrating as Parliament is, it's too precious to throw away."

"That's what mine says, too," Lana said.

"And mine," said Bugbite.

Eloquentia reached out and pinched a few grains off Lana's palm. When the deputy licked her fingers, Lana swooned. She raised her palm to her mouth and licked the rest of the yeast away. A cool, comfortable sense of well-being spread through her flesh. Parliament didn't matter anymore, but she was in her seat, in the absurd role assigned to her, trying her best to make it work.

Somewhere, miles away, the Speaker and the Maréchal were leaning over the Parliamentary records of customs, usage, and precedent, while the blood vessels in their eyes burst, one by one.

"I'm finally beginning to realize why this is all so damn intractable," Lana said, slumped in her seat, boneless as a garden slug. "There's nothing more stubborn than an asshole."

Bugbite giggled. She leaned over Lana's shoulder.

"You said *asshole*," she whispered.

"Go on, Lana," said Eloquentia.

"You called me by my name," Lana said to the deputy. "That's so sweet."

"Go on."

"Okay." Lana took a big breath. "Everything in Parliament depends on chitchat. Right?"

"I wouldn't call it that." Eloquentia's gaze was a little unfocused, but still serious.

"Yeah, I know. You have rules about who can chitchat when and where. It's all very formal." Lana waved both hands as if conducting an orchestra. "But what matters is stubbornness. Intractability. If you're willing to be the ultimate arse, you can get whatever you want. People will give way to you, even to the death."

Eloquentia opened her mouth as if to object. Her jaw hung there for a minute. Then it snapped shut.

"Maybe," she said reluctantly.

"Past death, actually," Lana said, eager. "Because didn't we just see Berkingmiddleshire spill her guts on the floor only an hour ago?" She pointed to the bloody brown smear on the far side of the floor.

"Four hours ago," said Bugbite.

"Has it been that long?" Lana cupped her hands on either side of her face. "How does anyone survive this? It's inhuman."

"I don't know," said Eloquentia. The yeast had taken full effect. The dancer drained out of her and she was just a woman, slouching in her seat like any mortal. "It shouldn't be so hard to agree. Why is everything so impossible?"

Bugbite sat on the back of the bench between them. Eloquentia's shoulder tipped toward Lana's. Their two heads rested in the fairy's lap.

"Shouldn't you be up with the scribes, BB?" Lana murmured.

"No, I need to take care of you. It's dangerous down here."

"Mmm," Lana agreed.

While the Speaker and the Maréchal deliberated endlessly, the fairies tucked their guns under their elbows and retreated into the rafters. The ruby fairy stayed behind, perched on the back of the Speaker's throne, her chin on her fist and her two golden guns across her knee. She tapped her heel against the upholstery, not in impatience, Lana thought, but to remind the two officials of the passing of time.

As day passed into night, more votes hung, tragically and intractably. The Hanging Man watched it all with his dead eyes.

The Speaker and the Maréchal were trying their best to change history. In the first vote, they allowed the deputies to vote at will, but that hadn't worked. For the second, they tried forming three voting parties again, but the deputies milled in confusion. For the third, they tried announcing one voting party and decreeing utter consensus, but most of the deputies refused to leave their seats. In the fourth, they went back to voting at will and hung.

When they returned to their bench after the fourth vote, Eloquentia rested her cheek on Bugbite's knee.

"I just want this all to end," she said. The fairy patted the deputy's hair.

"This ridiculous House can't agree on a blank piece of paper," said Lana.

The Speaker called out in her weak and strained voice. "The next Call for Decision is sponsored by the deputy from Dauphine-Provence."

Eloquentia looked desperate. She fumbled through her papers and grabbed a blank sheet.

"I remove the contents of my call." She stood and waved the blank sheet. "It is null. Surely, we can agree on nothing, so here is an opportunity for consensus."

The Maréchal banged the gavel. From atop the Speaker's throne, the ruby fairy leveled her guns at Eloquentia's head. The Speaker summoned the energy for something approaching a shout.

"I will remind the deputy from Dauphine-Provence that we must not find her in contempt of this august House."

Lana stepped in front of Eloquentia.

"Point of clarification, if you please, Madam Speaker?" she sang out.

"Dauphine-Provence has the floor," growled the Maréchal.

"*Qu'est-ce que tu fais?*" Eloquentia whispered. She kicked Lana's boot with the soft toe of her court slipper.

"Trust me," Lana whispered back.

"Yeah, trust her," Bugbite repeated.

"I cede the floor to the new deputy from Berkingmiddleshire. I believe her intentions are pure," Eloquentia said. "She's the only one in this whole House I can say that about."

This last bit she muttered under her breath as she sat, and thank goodness, because from the look in the ruby fairy's eye, she would have been shot.

Lana spread her arms wide, giving Ruby a bigger target.

"This officious House generally does its business in the language of fairykin. That makes sense, because Eurobabble includes hundreds of languages, and most of us want to understand each other, at least some of the time."

Lana slowly raised one finger as if about to make some kind of salient point—though what it might be she had no idea. She was pulling words out of her ass.

"Custom, usage, and precedent of this obtrusive House recognizes the validity of every language. Parliament puts no restrictions on the mother tongues spoken on this floor."

She was just guessing. But to emphasize her point, she gestured at the shining tiles of the Assembly Hall, making the most of the reach of her long arms and trying to look very serious indeed. If she pretended her babble made sense, maybe others would take it for a given?

"Good one," whispered Bugbite. "Keep going. You can do this."

"Philosophers and theorists through the ages, from antiquity all the way through to this morning, agree on one thing." Lana tapped the blade of one palm into her open hand. She was running out of confident gestures and would have to start repeating herself soon. "Not all languages are verbal. For instance, deaf women speak in sign language."

Lana signed the one sentence she knew: *Would you like to come to bed with me?* Somewhere across the floor, a deputy guffawed.

"And some languages have no written form. That makes them no less a language and no less valid in this complacent House." She swept her arm wide in Eloquentia's direction. "Madam Speaker, the language in which my respected colleague from Dauphine-Provence prepared her Call for Decision has no written form. That's why the sheet is blank."

"Lana," Eloquentia whispered. "Be careful."

Lana put her hand behind her back and gave the deputy a thumbs-up.

"The language she uses precludes lies. And no, my colleagues, you deputies, you sweet and precious fairykin, Madam Speaker, Madam Maréchal, guards, pages, scribes, and librarians, I am not exaggerating." She swept both arms up to the ceiling, gesturing at the Hanging Man. "In the language of dance, truth is not only essential, anything other than truth is impossible. The body does not lie."

Lana pressed her palms together and opened them as if blessing the deputies.

"This stupendous House cannot vote on a blank page. But the page is not blank. It is unwritten."

"What's the difference?" someone shouted from the back of the room.

"La députée de Dauphine-Provence will show you the difference. I cede the floor to her."

Eloquentia stood. She dropped the deputy's robes from her shoulders, kicked off her slippers, and floated down the steps to the floor. Her shoulders were loose, the column of her spine pliant as a reed. When she lifted her arms, it wasn't like one of Lana's ridiculous, playing-for-time pantomime gestures; it was truth.

The dancer took possession of the center of the room and turned. No big movements, no leaps or jumps, just turned in a circle over and over again as the lamplight played on her peony-pink gown. At first, the deputies shifted in their seats, clearly unsettled, but Eloquentia's attitude of gravity and concentration spread through the room like a spell. Soon, everyone was breathing in the same rhythm. And the fairies—the fairies were descending from the ceiling.

They perched on bench backs, wings open and resting. The eyes of their butterfly markings seemed to watch the dancer, as much as every other pair in the room. And when Eloquentia first made the barest variation on her slow and continual spin, each and every fairy sighed along with the humans.

Eloquentia picked up a box—no box, in reality, but a box made visible in the imagination. She moved it from one spot to another, then picked up another to place on top. And another and another until in the center of the floor was a tower of boxes, a ziggurat. And then her movements quickened. She spun around the tower, worshipping it, protecting it.

Was it a natal tower, with a fairy on top, waiting to grant conception wishes? No. And yes. Was it a house built with sweat and love to protect families from the wet and cold? No, and yes. Was it a great institution made top-heavy by custom, usage, and precedent? Yes, yes, yes. Tottering, certainly. Vulnerable, too. Taken for granted, but the peace it promised no less precious.

For all that Eloquentia's dance had begun controlled and minimalist, it ended in raw emotion. If any woman could convey passion for a stack of imaginary boxes, the dancer did, and better, she made everyone watching care about it, too, and everything it symbolized.

Sweating, her hair webbed in tangles over her face, Eloquentia dropped to her knees. Not a word was said, not a breath taken until she stood and retook her seat.

"The deputies will cross the floor to vote at will," said the Speaker.

Lana took Eloquentia's hand and led her to the Ayes. Bugbite flew with them. As in the previous votes, there was no way to judge the numbers from the floor, but Lana saw something that surprised her.

It wasn't only humans gathering in the Ayes but fairies,

too. Usually during a vote, they'd be flying overhead to ratify the enumeration. Not this time. Not a single fairy in the air. They'd joined the vote, each and every beautiful one of them.

"The Ayes are unanimous," the Speaker said. "The Call for Decision passes."

Howls. Cheers. Arms in the air and caps launched across the room. Glee and joy, and not only from the humans but from the fairies, too. Lana had seen a fairy smile. Bugbite smiled, but she was exceptional. This was different. All the fairies were smiling now, laughing, too, and congratulating their human friends.

Eloquentia was still sweating when Lana took her in her arms. She hadn't put her deputy robes back on, and the pink satin of her gown was stained dark along the neckline. The dancer fit under Lana's chin, just as Lana had dreamed of. But something was missing.

"BB," Lana said. "Do you want to come here?"

When she stretched out an arm toward her friend, the fairy didn't hesitate. She dove into the embrace, laughing. She planted an awkward kiss on the corner of Lana's mouth, then turned to Eloquentia and kissed her, too, managing a bit better with her aim.

"I will get better with practice," Bugbite said, and kissed them both again.

17

Lana inherited Berkingmiddleshire's rooms, and the digs were quite roomy. But even if they'd been small, they would have had to make do, because Bugbite moved in permanently, and Eloquentia, after visiting on the first night, never left.

The small house stood at the very top of the allée, where the stairs curved toward the abbey. From one side of their upper-floor bedroom, they could watch comings and go-ings through a wide window, and on the other side, three sturdy shuttered panes gave a triptych view of wide sand, gleaming ocean, and the inexorable tides that changed the one into the other.

"Will you be happy here?" asked Eloquentia as she spread cherry jam on a rusk for her breakfast. "You didn't choose this life."

"I can be happy anywhere," Lana said.

From the seat on the windowsill, Bugbite nodded. She nipped the stamen off a massive daylily.

"Lana has a talent for happiness. It's a great gift."

"Thank you, BB." Lana was quite touched.

"And we're not letting you go anyway. So you have no choice," the fairy added.

"If you are happy anywhere, how can your lovers know they're important? Must we take it on faith?"

"You can take it on demonstration." Lana slid her hand up Eloquentia's hip and dipped in for a jam-flavored kiss. She nipped the dancer's lower lip for emphasis.

Their seaward windows didn't afford a view of the port or the road that crossed the sands to the gate, but the traffic moving up and down the allée testified that Parliament was coming to life again. People were coming back, shops reopening, cooks and maids, laundrywomen and carpenters all returning to a House renewed. Strengthened in purpose, cynicism expelled—at least for the time being.

Votes were counted in a strict majority, and whether it be Yea or Nay, Parliament was working again.

If Lana slept through the majority of sessions, she had good reason. The three of them were staying up late each night. For the joy of love, oh yes, first and foremost—but for politics, too.

Bugbite, Lana, and Eloquentia were brewing a Call for Decision that would bring fairies into Parliament as deputies. No more would the government operate as if fairies had no role but enforcers, essential, but always separate. No, they would participate. And if it made them grumpy, made them hate humans, well, that would be no change.

Lana drew Bugbite's feet into her lap and kneaded her toes. Her whiskers shivered. Eloquentia took another bite of her cherry rusk and chewed it with great pleasure.

"When all three of us are deputies, will we always vote alike?" Lana asked her fairy friend, now most beloved.

A frosting of pollen dusted Bugbite's cheeks. She wiped it away with the back of her hand.

"If you're smart," she said, looking up into Lana's face with a fond smile, "you'll vote like me. A fairy knows what's best."

Acknowledgments

A grateful thank you to my editor Ellen Datlow for keenness, sensitivity, and warmth. Thank you to Irene Gallo and Emily Goldman at Tordotcom for giving my work a loving home. Early readers (actually, listeners) Margo MacDonald, Titus Androgynous, and the late Linda Carson (much, much missed) provided laughter and encouragement. Jeffe Kennedy supported me daily via chat (how did writers ever work without it?). My agent, Hannah Bowman, deserves all thanks for always being awesome. And as always, thank you to my dear wife, Alyx; you make the impossible real.

About the Author

© Kristy Boyce

KELLY ROBSON lives in downtown Toronto with her wife, writer A. M. Dellamonica. Her novelette "A Human Stain" won the 2018 Nebula Award, and her time-travel adventure *Gods, Monsters, and the Lucky Peach* won the 2019 Aurora Award and was a finalist for the Hugo, Nebula, Theodore Sturgeon, and Locus Awards. Kelly's first short story collection, *Alias Space and Other Stories*, was published in 2021. Find her on Twitter and Instagram.

TOR·COM

Science fiction. Fantasy. The universe.

And related subjects.

*

More than just a publisher's website, *Tor.com*
is a venue for **original fiction, comics,** and
discussion of the entire field of SF and fantasy,
in all media and from all sources. Visit our site
today—and join the conversation yourself.